CN00866805

BEI

ROC

HAR

PAULIE'S WEB

Paulie's Web

Wendy Robertson

Room To Write

First Published on Kindle 2011
Revised Edition Published 2013
ISBN 10 1492104078
ISBN 13 978149210104070

DEDICATION

For all the women I met behind bars with the hope that in *Paulie's Web*, they will hear the whisper of their own voices. And for Avril Joy, with whom I worked in prison. Avril has, through the years, given me a very special key to understanding the power and impact of events on the inside.

ACKNOWLEDGMENTS

As well as the women I met in HMP Low Newton, I would like to acknowledge all the people who facilitated my life-changing residency, especially the officers on the wing who were helpful and kind to this stranger. And thank you to Jane Peers for the wonderful cover drawing from *Why Am I Running?* Thanks also to Clive and Pauline Hopwood of the Writers in Prison Network for their cheerful support..

I am profoundly grateful to Governor Mike Kirby who was forward-looking and compassionate with the women – and the staff – in his care. I was especially lucky because Mike Kirby read and enjoyed good fiction.

WENDY ROBERTSON

ABOUT THE AUTHOR

Wendy Robertson has written popular and well-reviewed novels for adults and children and a memoir of her writing life, *The Romancer*. For five years from 1999 she was writer-in residence in a woman's prison. Now as well as writing a novel each year she writes a popular writer's blog
A Life Twice Tasted at
http://www.lifetwicetasted.blogspot.co.uk/

She says *of Paulie's Web.* '*It has taken me some years to digest the extremities of my experience in prison and to write my novel as true fiction in a way that pays tribute to the women I met while working there. If, by the by,* **Paulie's Web** *goes some way to cracking the absurd stereotypes of women in prison this will be an extra delight. While there are dark elements in the novel I make no apologies for its ultimately optimistic tone which is a true reflection of the humour, stoicism and kindness that I witnessed in my prison experience.*'

WENDY ROBERTSON

1 PAULIE GETS OUT

Paulie: It took me twenty three years of fairly chaotic living to get myself into jail and six years to get out. Some say I'm lucky that it only took me six years to get out of that surreal place called prison. Some say I was stupid. It would have been just four years if I'd admitted doing the vile thing they sentenced me for. As it is I served six of a nine year stretch. Without the campaign I'd have clocked the full nine years.

I didn't serve my time all in one jail, of course. They move you around so you don't get bored. So I've been told. But really they move you around to keep you teetering on the edge: uncertain, helpless. That's how they like you. They know that a person is more malleable in that state. Uncertainty. The magazines are full of it. Potted psychotherapy, earnest psychobabble. The fact is, I've done time in a few different jails since they dispersed the five of us from Brontë house after the hair riot.

I complained all the times about them keeping me teetering on the edge: I put in five apps, complaining about just how bad it is to have someone say, 'Get your gear, you're going.' In a second. No notice. Just 'Get your gear, you're going.' Five apps! They all tell me - except for the governors (who more circumspect language) - that it's just what people like me deserve. Dangerous people should be kept teetering. It turns out you're a piece of hot property to be moved from one warehouse to the other to prevent conflagration.

Quite right too! That's what I'd say to them. Quite right! In the end I'd always agree with them. I'd seem sympathetic to their dilemma. It's hard to take issue with someone who agrees with you, however insincere they are. Have you noticed that? The only thing I didn't agree with in those days was that I'd actually done that terrible thing.

In the end I was the very last to make my way out: - the last, that is, of that first group of women in the van. I got out some years after Queenie, Christine, Maritza and Lilah. These were amazing women; good women in their own way. Of course I've met a few interesting women in my six years within those walls. Some of them were good, some of them were bad; a couple of them were really very bad - women whose dark fame has spread far and wide with names as familiar as royalty – celebrities for very dark reasons.

Jail is a world on its own: that microcosm of life behind bars has been another higher education for me. My years in prison have been my master's degree in weird-world living, in the surreal dramas of time and space in the geography of the soul, the topography of the human psyche. Gulliver never travelled this far nor did he ever meet such strange creatures, in or out of uniform.

But it's those first weeks that remain unique, very special for me - those first hours in the white van (which they actually did call the paddy wagon), and those first weeks at Brontë House. That was when I spent time with four women - Queenie, Maritza, Lilah and Christine. In their company during those first weeks I was transformed from one kind of woman into another; more peculiarly loved and loving – in fact a more surviving kind of creature. Those four women listened with me to that night-time roar with the same dank fear in their hearts as they heard the very worst of humanity spit itself out into the dry air. I've heard the night roars many times since, but never with that same painful, fearful apprehension as those first weeks.

These day, of course, everyone is telling me how lucky I am, managing to get out against all the odds. The women, the officers, my brief, my psych - everyone tells me that.

I was sentenced to nine years for my serious offence which involved fire. But it seems, now, that it was an *unsafe* conviction. At my original trial they were still determined to show that I'd burned Charlie because years before they'd never been convinced I hadn't burnt my father. That fact, added to the circumstantial evidence in the night of the fire, plus the feelings out there in the community at the time, made sure that the jury found me guilty.

Remember? All that spitting outrage during the trial. About the vetting of teachers and how had I got into the classroom alongside the innocent children? Were there no records of the original fire? They screamed it. Screamed it. One opportunistic journalist interviewed Mrs. Townshend, my toby-jug head-teacher, and her words spread like wildfire. Another journo dug even deeper than that and talked to the creepy Miss Saltbrace, who wept buckets over the children she'd handed over to me at my first school. Crocodile tears, they were. Saltbrace should have wept for all those children she herself had taught in twenty five years.

It was a surprise when Maritza told me - one night in

7

Association at Bronte House - that Miss Saltbrace had taught her when she was little. The old boot had called her a thief in front of all the class. Sweet little Maritza! We spent the whole of that session calling Saltbrace a cow, a wolfess, and even better names than that. We laughed very, very loud, (the way you learn to in prison, to be visible), and wished the woman dead. I have to say I was a bit taken aback at the energy, the sheer power with which our little Maritza bad mouthed Saltbrace. She was a dark horse, was that Maritza.

So, as you can see, now at last I was getting out. You'll have seen the newspaper articles about it. Pauline Smith released. *Sad miscarriage of justice* ... *Inadequate representation* ... *Lost young life*... Crocodile tears spilt all over the place.

Coming out of the gate that morning was the coming-of-age of all time. The Governor – not a bad bloke - fixed it up for me to come through the gate twenty four hours before the fact was made public. All smiling and helpful, the governor was. Apologising for the system, really. I was pleased. Couldn't stand the thought of those hacks getting the hots over me going through all this. Journalism! I could write it better myself. The stuff they wrote originally gave me nightmares for years. Of course they've changed their tune, now – whistling a very different song. Some of the reporters who originally came to talk to me seemed to be getting off on it. Men and woman, high colour, hands jammed in pockets, fast voices and all that. Telling me it was only fair that I should tell my story.

An organisation called Gaia wanted to send someone to meet me on the day I came out. Clearly they wanted to clasp me to their bosom and make me feel safe. But I turned them down. I know how to keep myself safe. I'm not daft. No way I'm one set of jailers for another. Find me doing that. Fuck that! Oh God! I must watch that, the language. Keep it for the page. Inmate-speak is too easy. I've got to lose that to slide properly into the world.

Paulie Smith, now aged twenty-nine, moves sideways in on the world - cautiously, like a crab...

The gates roll and grind closed behind me, and I am here, the grey sky exploding fireworks of light over my head. I am drunk on space, incontinent with light. I open my mouth wide to gulp in fresh, clean, free air. I unzip the neck of my anorak to let this air in on my body, waving my arms to let it flow to my elbows, my armpits.

Some body! This body's is a good stone and a half heavier than when I came in six years ago. My hair is long now, down my back in a long plait. When I went in, my hair was cropped short. On that first day Queenie chuckled at my boy's cut, didn't she? Compared me with some boy she knew whose father took his clippers right across his head like a convict. Some kid in one of her classes.

She'd been a teacher, had Queenie. Like me.

2 QUEENIE AND THE WATERMAN

Queenie's hat was always cocked at a cheeky angle. She had always been very particular about her appearance. Her eyes embraced those about her with an engaging confidence. She was extravagant with her perfume: this month *Rive Gauche*, next month *Je T 'Adore* - all gifts from her niece, Janine, who was what they call a Flight Attendant. Queenie relished those words. *Flight Attendant*. Such glamour.

Janine had always kept her Auntie Queenie supplied with perfume and with liquor for her glass-fronted cocktail cabinet with the let-down shelf. The interior light - such an innovation when Queenie bought it in the Sixties – had not worked in recent years and the mirror-back and glass shelves were rarely dusted.

The first time the terrible thing happened Queenie committed herself voluntarily to hospital; she praised the nurses and psychiatrists for their close care, despite her stifled resentment at their calling her *Queenie*, and not *Miss Pickering*. Queenie was a nice name to be sure, given to her by her neighbours at the age of six when she was May Queen in her village. After that her given name of Vivian was rarely used.

But only Janine and two or three old friends were allowed to call her Queenie. To everyone else she was always *Miss Pickering*. The world called her Miss Pickering.

Two generations of schoolchildren in her village had called her Miss Pickering. Even when two of them - grown up now and equipped with mobile phones and Ford Escorts - came upon her one midnight as she walked through the woodland, clad only in her petticoat and an armour-like brassière, muttering lines from the poet John Clare: even these two likely lads called her Miss Pickering.

It was the lads' kindness and distress which made her, that first time, decide she must seek help at the hospital. In the hospital the doctor gave her some pills so that when she got back home she no longer saw the Water Man in the woods, rising, dripping pond weed and silvery fish, fairies dancing at his shoulder: the Water Man who smelled of almonds and honey wine.

She endured this for quite a while before she decided to leave off the pills 'just for a day or so'. The first day she sat back, walked around and waited for the sparkle to come back in her life, for the Water Man to stride the earth again. The second day she put on her hat at its cocky angle, splashed herself with *Je t'Adore* and set forth into the village.

Ah, wonderful! The colours were brighter and the noises were louder, harmonious and clashing at the same time. People swept by her in warm beams of light. The buses roared and took on the aspects of scarlet tigers. The cars were insects, bright as jewels.

As she exclaimed and laughed at all this beauty people on the pavement gave her a wide berth. As the days rolled by she began to go further and further afield, to drink in all the beauty, to allow the Great Ones to come before her. She would return to the little house later and later. But sometimes she would be just about ready to get into bed when the beauty of the world outside would call her again and she just had to get up and go outside to bathe in its light.

One night she was actually in bed when some lines from the lovely Browning popped into her head.

"Thou, Soul, explorest -
Though in a trembling rapture - space
Immeasurable! Shrubs, turned trees,
Trees that touch heaven, support its frieze
Studded with moon and sun and star."
She chanted the words again and again,

She chanted them as she raced through her back door, through the wicket space in her fence, on, on, towards the woodland. *Trees that touch Heaven ... Trees that touch Heaven.*

Ali Smith and George Onyatt, returning from a late drink at The Green Tree pub, saw her figure before them, fluttering in a long night dress. 'There she goes again, Ali!' George Onyatt gave chase and soon caught up with her. 'Come on, Queenie!' he said, his voice reasonable. 'This is no way to go on. No way at all.' He grabbed her arm.

She lifted her other hand and whammed her fist into his face. 'Miss Pickering to you, George Onyatt! Miss Pickering to you and to your father as well. Your father was a poor, mewling boy when he was in my class.'

He caught her hand in his, tight. 'Come on, Queenie.' He sneered. 'Queenie's good enough for a mad old bat any day.' That was when she brought his hand to her mouth and bit it, sinking her teeth to the bone.

Howling, he let her go.

She stood still before him, and then looked at Ali Smith who had now caught up with them. 'My name is Miss Pickering,' she said. 'You know that, don't you

Alistair?'

That time Queenie was sectioned and in the hospital they gave her the pills that again took away her visions of the giant trees and stars and the Water Man. She was meek, very good, in the hospital. She helped with the tea rounds, taught a young girl and a young boy to read, and stayed tucked up in her bed all night.

When they had a case conference the professionals decided that Queenie Pickering was a prime candidate for Care in the Community, now not only fashionable but compulsory. Her house with its dusty cocktail cabinet was sold. In a rare soft moment she signed the cottage over to Janine, who had sold it and gone off to build a new life for herself and her boyfriend Roger, in the depths of Canada.

But there was this thing called Sheltered Housing now. Queenie - for everyone called her Queenie now - Queenie could live there and the nurse could call every week to see that she was taking her medication. Everything would be Hunky Dory. Wasn't that how Care in the Community worked?

After a week there, Queenie walked out of the Sheltered Housing. She put on her hat - not so smart now - piled all her most precious things in three carrier bags, and caught the long distance bus to the edges of a large town where they would never find her. Best to lie low like Brer Rabbit, she thought. Best to lie low. As she settled down in the bus she knew she would find the gleaming Water Man there. He was everywhere, so he would be in the city. And the sky in that place would be studded with the pearly moon, the golden sun and the silver stars. And there again the trees would stride the earth.

3 AN ORDINARY LIFE

Maritza: Squat like a frog and breathing words the child Maritza didn't understand, this weird woman who ruled the household. She was generous in provision and peculiarly mean in execution. After the child had finished her cup of tea, the frog women would wash the single cup and saucer by filling the saucer only with scalding water then turning the cup in it until every surface had been covered. 'Saves water,' she croaked.

The woman never touched Maritza, but only rarely looked her in the eyes.

The little house in the dale smelled of washing and baking, bleach and bootblack. The air, enclosed behind sealed doors and tight windows, was dry and hot. The desert heat was maintained by the fire which roared up the chimney, stoked through the day by the buckets of coal which the woman threw onto the brick shelf behind the fire and raked down, bit by bit, as the day ticked on.

It was in this house that the Maritz became easy about stealing. She would take sixpences left carelessly for her on polished surfaces; she filched sweets spilling temptingly towards her out of crackling packets; she pocketed biscuit and cakes that hung their tempting sweet scents on the air. The stealing started when she was searching the small house for a small panda bear which had gone missing from the other house in which they lived, in another town where they had lived with her father.

The woman told her that her mother was away 'packing up that house': packing it up into boxes and then into a van. A whole house into a van! Maritza worried about the bricks and the iron gate. How would they get into a van?

His shoes. Her mother would be packing up her father's shoes, which had creases where the leather had moulded itself on his feet. His feet were long and narrow and he believed in wearing tight shoes. He once told Maritza that 'A decent shoe needs to be worn in on your foot.' So he had left his mark in them.

Her father had been very light on his feet and one Christmas they had all danced to music tinkling out from a new record player. Her mother danced with her brother, her father with Maritza. They swirled around and round in the small front room till they fell laughing in a heap on to the sofa.

Now her mother would be packing his black suit with the waistcoat: the suit he danced in. Maritza remembered seeing it on the back of the bedroom chair. And his Brylcream. She had seen it on the dressing table, half-used, still delved with the mark of his fingers.

Maritza and her brother had arrived at the little cottage with single suitcase between them. They were to stay there while their mother packed up the old house. The weird frog woman and her husband had welcomed them with self-righteous smiles and restrained nods.

Nobody touched you, in this house. The child Maritza thought that no one would touch her ever again. But her father had touched her. When they walked along together his fingers - too long to be contained by the small hand he was grasping - would slip up the sleeve of her cardigan. You could climb on his knee and smell his cigarette smoke and feel his long arms about you as he read his paper.

When the door clicked shut as your mother went out to work you relished the sense of ease that rippled through the house. It was as though the whole house, as well as those in it, breathed out. Now, you could climb again onto his knee. Or stand by the spurting cooker and watch his bony hand stir the porridge with a wooden spoon. Maritza, in later days, could never remember the taste of that porridge: just the bony hand, stirring.

Here in the narrow cottage the people didn't mention the stealing. Oh no. Not immediately. Later on, the frog woman's son did mention it, in the child's hearing, as though she weren't there. 'Money missing again in the house but you ain't supposed to say,' he hissed to his friend who was mending a bicycle inner tube in a scummy bowl of water in the yard. 'Thieves about! Beware.' He looked through the spokes of the wheel at Maritza lurking in the doorway.

Maritza didn't keep the money. She just moved it to a different place: down the back of the toilet, the arms of chairs; behind curtains on windowsills; or under the bedroom carpet. She didn't keep the sweets either. She climbed up on chairs and put them in lines, marching along the picture rails. The cakes she crumbled into the garden borders, stubbing them into the ground with her foot till the golden crumbs had blended with the soil. She never ate one single cake.

She didn't know why she did this.

Not a word was said by the grownups around her

about these habits of hers; not even to her mother when she finally arrived with two bulging black suitcases. Maritza's inner eye retained the image of those cases for many years. They were made of false leather, rubbed and cracked at the corners. Her mother arrived sitting upfront in the delivery van that had been driven all the way from their old house in a faraway city.

Her mother's stout figure shimmered with the last scents of the house and the last shreds of Maritza's father. Maritza wanted to plunge into her, to bury her head in the hard round breasts encased in an armoured brassiére. She clambered up into the van, onto her mother's knee and sat stiffly there, squashed in by her brother. Their new house, only a mile down the road, was half as big as their old one, where they had lived with their father. This one still smelled of the blind man who had died there and it had only one cold tap.

Maritza watched the men unload the van. Trying not to blink in case she missed anything, Maritza watched her mother break open the boxes and unpack all their things: jumpers, coats, cardigans and knickers; towels and curtains tied around with string like bulging corpses.

She was hopeful at first.

But the black and white panda bear was not there either. After the men had unloaded the goods and were clear of the house Maritza's mother lit her first cigarette and kneeled down to light a fire in the black grate. The rising smoke puffing into the room made a halo around her head. Maritza's brother took a rediscovered ball outside to play with in the yard, screwing himself up to ignore the boys who were sitting on the wall, watching.

Now Maritza set about looking again in the boxes

and the leatherette cases, the bags and the sacks. She looked everywhere but nowhere could she find the panda bear. Her mother sat smoking her fourth cigarette and stared into the fire. Her face was white and pale. She looked blankly at Maritza when she asked the question.

'Panda?' She took a long drag on her cigarette. 'Panda? What are you saying? Your father's dead and you ask me about a panda?'

After that time the child, then the adult Maritza, kept on looking for the panda but only within the safe confines of her dreams. Every morning when she woke up she would stoke up the memory of her frantic dream searches: how she had swung open creaking cupboard doors, dragged out drawers, peered at the back of searing fires, how she had peered into in the cold spaces between the windows and the glass.

Looking, always looking. In the dream Maritza was always convinced she'd find the panda, that he would be in the next box, the next bag, but she never did. And when she woke up the panda was still not there.

In this new home which had only one cold tap, she had to sleep in the same bed as her mother. Each night she could feel her mother's misery seeping into her, leeching across the woven threads of the grey blankets into her own arms, her shoulders, the lines of her calves. The sour scent of her mother's pain was on her pillow.

After she started her new school Maritza started to steal in a more determined way: sweets and chocolate bars from shops; pencils and rubbers and mittens from the other children at school. Once, she took a red mackintosh hooded cape with a hood from a peg in the cloakroom. She realised she couldn't wear it so she hid it in the coal-house, under the coals, and then later stuffed it in the bin under the ashes from the coal fire. She watched the bin man take it and tip it into the wide mouth of his wagon: slimy streaks of red showed through the rubbish.

Miss Saltbrace, the teacher in her new school, reminded Maritza of the weird frog woman. She did not like it when this new child got her sums right by using the wrong method, the method she'd been taught at the other, faraway school. The teacher's voice would ping off the glass windows of the partition. 'Where did you learn this? Where did you learn this way?' The question was a reproof and required no response.

There came a day when Maritza did respond. 'Please, Miss Saltbrace, I learned it on the planet Jupiter.'

The painful strokes of the cane burned her hand. The pain was welcome. Clean. This was the first direct, passionate contact with another human being since her father died: since before he went into hospital. When she reckoned up, the pain was worth it.

One day they had a visitor in the classroom: a young woman who had frizzy hair and bright green eyes behind round glasses. Her long legs were encased in glass nylons, making her legs shine like a snail trail. The teacher beamed at the newcomer. 'Miss Pomfret. Welcome to Class Three!' There was some muttering between them, some business about the groups and the work in progress. Then Miss Saltbrace surveyed the classroom, her spectacles glittering. 'However I must warn you, Miss Pomfret that it is our misfortune to have a thief in the classroom. Haven't we children?'

'Yes, Miss Saltbrace!' That fluting chorus, that anxious agreement.

Miss Saltbrace's eyes settled on Maritza. 'Come out Maritza Turner,' she said. 'Come out! Here is our thief, Miss Pomfret. You must watch this one. Keep your eyes skinned.'

Ever obedient, Maritza got to her feet and stumbled forward. The teacher's hand dug painfully in her shoulder. 'This is the one to watch, Miss Pomfret. Remember the name. Maritza Turner. The one to watch.'

The green eyes that surveyed her through the glasses were clouded with some feeling, some doubt. The young woman's hand came forward and the child reached out to grasp it. 'I'm sure you won't steal from me, will you?' said Miss Pomfret softly.

The teacher pulled Maritza away, out of the visitor's grasp. 'Don't be too sure,' she snapped. 'Don't you be too sure!'

Maritza wriggled away from the teacher's hand and made her way back to her seat. Halfway down the aisle she stopped and turned round to face the newcomer. 'Miss…' she said.

Green Eyes smiled. 'Yes?' she said.

'Do you make cakes? You know, those things called Pomfret cakes?' she asked.

Miss Saltbrace's face filled with thunder and her mouth opened to roar. But Miss Pomfret smiled. The clouds melted. The storm was pre-empted. 'D'you know, Maritza Turner, I wish I'd a penny for every time someone has said that to me?'

Then the class, given such open permission, laughed out loud. Miss Saltbrace shrugged, picked up her handbag with its precious cigarettes (filter-tipped) and its silver lighter. 'Well,' she drawled. 'See what you can make of this lot, Miss Pomfret. And good luck to you.'

Years afterwards the girl behind the counter at Fenwicks reminded Maritza Molloy of that student teacher, all those years ago. This girl too had green eyes and bushy hair, but her hair was dyed black as ink and tied back with a flowered scrunchie. Her nails were long and red and she smelled of five perfumes.

'Not your colour, madam, not at all,' the girl drawled. 'Try the Translucent Honey. Your skin is very light. Try Translucent Honey, madam.' Then she went across to speak to another customer. When she came back, Maritza, (three Translucent Honeys safely tucked away in her bag now), handed the fourth jar back to the girl. 'I'm not too sure, dear,' she said. 'I'll leave it for now.'

The girl's green eyes narrowed. 'Would you like another brand Madam?' she snapped. 'This Max Factor one is even lighter. More a mousse than a cream.'

'I'll just leave it,' Maritza said firmly. She pulled her gloves, smoothed them on her wrists and wandered back, very slowly, between the counters and through the swing doors at the other end. Once outside she stood still on the pavement, breathing in and out very slowly to allow her heartbeat to come back to normal and the tingle in her fingers to subside. Then she strolled along to the florist on the corner and paid ten pounds for a hand-rolled bunch of lilies and tulips. They would go on the dining room windowsill and catch the morning light very nicely. She did like flowers around the house.

Waltzing, waltzing to spritely music: her mother and father, herself and her brother. Herself and Miss Saltbrace. Miss Saltbrace and Miss Pomfret. The panda and Miss

21

Pomfret, the black parts of the panda's fur gleaming like liquorice pomfret cakes. Her father and Miss Pomfret, twirling away. Then all of them reflected in the translucent ellipses of Miss Pomfret's glasses which protected those bright green eyes.   Her mother and brother.   Herself all alone, twirling. Dancing. Light as a feather

4
GETAWAY

Paulie: The taxi isn't there by the prison gates. The Governor told me he'd fixed up a taxi. I'd pictured it standing there, like in the movies. A long black limo. I'd seen myself hopping in the back and making my getaway. But that's clearly not going to happen. At least there are no reporters, no cameras here, like there will be tomorrow, which is my official getaway day.

So I have to wait here with all my worldly goods in two bulky carrier bags. At least I'm not carrying my books. I had special permission from the Governor to post parcels of books to Mr John Kebler the psych. Those books and these two bursting carriers: my worldly goods.

It's cold. My breath escapes from my mouth and sits on the air like smoke, then drifts across to thread its way through the noisy chirrup of bird song and weaves on down through the dusty winter hedge. Then this breath of my mouth, this free breath in the free air, drifts from branch to branch to settle with a dying fall on the discarded crackling bags which once held crisps and condoms, cigarettes and fizzy pop, apples and sly wraps.

This brings Queenie to my mind. Here am I, just like Queenie: waddling along the road with carrier bags. But no hat! At l east I'm not wearing a hat. I lean forward to look along the road to see if the taxi's actually coming. I see them watching me, those shadowy figures in the gate office - uniforms with round heads. Before me the long road snakes away into the dizzying distance. It is very empty, so I hunch my shoulders and set off to walk. In the last six years I've not walked any distance longer than ten corridor yards. This narrow road, this suburban route, stretches out for me like the pathway to Mars.

I've been walking for three minutes when a taxi draws up beside me. The driver must be used to pale-faced figures laden with carriers on this road. 'Railway station?' he says.

I throw my bags into the taxi. 'Yeah,' I say. 'Railway station.' He glances at me through the taxi window and I clock the wolfish glance, which reminds me of Bernie, Charlie's uncle. 'Straight back on the rob?' he says.

I settle back in the seat and watch the St Christopher swinging in the middle of the dashboard. 'Oh, yes. Nothing like a bit of grafting to get your blood up,' I say.

****

A take a train journey, then a second taxi from the station to drop me in the city, in Northumberland Street, beside Fenwick's. I stand on the pavement for a few minutes, rocked by the raging noise of traffic, the tramp of feet, the rustle of people ebbing and flowing, the roar of everyone shouting their business to each other or into their mobile phones. The brightness of the clothing, the primary colours, the tangle of arms and heads and legs: all this hurts my eyes. I am dazzled by the brilliant shine of words on fascias above the shops.

A man in the middle of the road stands juggling with fluffy panda bears. He wears the half-colours of a harlequin; his face is still and white like a clown. As he juggles a crowd of youngsters surge around him. He repeats rhymes and verses in a velvet growl. The children – aged seven, eight and nine, perhaps - shrug off the restraining hands of their mothers as they lean forward to drink in his magic. As for myself I'm intoxicated by the sleek hair, the round faces, and the bright eyes of these children. I've not seen anything this young, this fresh, for six years. I could weep with the promise in those bright faces. I want to weep for the children, for the child in me. She is lost now, gone forever, that child.

5 KISSING COUSINS

Christine: Christine Cazelet was taken into care at the age of eleven because her mother would not listen to her pleas to stop her cousin Seamus Bates baby-sitting for her and her sister Sallyanne on Saturday nights, when their mother went clubbing and their father went to play snooker.

After the thing first happened Christine kept her mouth tight shut for eighteen months, wary of Seamus' threat to kill her if she spoke out, if she told on him. He would kill her, he said, his eyes gleaming, but only after he'd killed young Sallyanne before her very eyes. He told her that he would make her little sister bleed to death like a stuck pig before her very eyes.

Cousin Seamus had this nice, lilting voice. Christine was forced to wait for him to stop singing lullabies to little Sallyanne in her bedroom. He sang to her to make sure she was fast asleep. Then Christine could hear his soft footfall as he crept along to her bedroom. That was when he did that terrible thing to her, stifling her groans with his hands as he pumped away. She tried to pretend she wasn't there. But she was there.

Christine couldn't tell her mother any of it. Christine couldn't tell her mother how Seamus pretended to be kind, saying that it always hurt at first, and every girl learned this terrible thing from someone who loved them, before they could grow up and go into the world and let strangers do it.

She would look around in school and wonder who else was learning this savage lesson. Which other girl was enduring this, amongst her own teddy bears and her own Sindy dolls, her own plasticine and paints? Three or four times each week Christine would beg her mother not to go out on a Saturday night.

Saturday night would find Mrs. Cazelet clicking down the street in her high heels Mrs. Cazelet would laugh with her friends, talking about how their Christine was getting so clingy these days. She had such a hard week working in the shop and Saturday night was her reward. She didn't drink much, but dancing! She loved to dance. It was such a relief, dancing, giving yourself up to the music. She so loved to dance. Her husband, Len, had his snooker, and she had her dancing. It was only fair.

And she would always mention that they were so lucky with young Seamus. He made the girls their supper and young Sallyanne idolised him. 'Just like Christine did, until she started this thing about wanting me there all the time. Getting too clingy by half.'

Before she went out Mrs. Cazelet would unpeel Christine's clinging hands and say, 'Stop it, will you? Stop! You're too old for this.'

Mrs. Cazelet laughed one night with Seamus. 'I don't know what's happening to our Christine, Seamus. Begrudges me my night out, little monster.'

That night Seamus called Christine a monster several times and told her that if she made a fuss on a Saturday night again he would kill Sallyanne and throw her body over the cliff into the sea. Her head would split open on the rocks. And the blood would pour out. After that, Christine stopped making any fuss at all. Her mother petted her, said what a good girl she was now, and brought her a new Sindy doll.

As time went on Christine was quieter in the house and quieter at school. One day in the toilets she heard a girl telling another about a trip to the cinema with her father and her cousin, Declan. 'Your cousin Declan,' said Christine, coming up to stand too near the girl, 'Do you like him?'

The girl looked at her, hard. 'Yeah. He's all right. He's a big laugh.' She took a step back. 'He's brilliant.'

'Does he … Does he…?' Christine said desperately. 'Does he do things to you?'

The girl laughed. 'Do things? He ties me to a tree when we play cowboys.'

'Does he do other things?' Christine persisted.

The girl pushed her so hard she fell against a basin. 'What're you talking about?' she shouted. Then she grabbed her friend. 'Come on, gerrout of here. That lass is mad, talking dirty stuff. That Christine Cazelet is mad.'

Their steps rang hollowly on the tiles, and the door clanged behind them. Christine looked at herself in the mirror and saw her own anxious face, wide-browed and large-nosed. She laid her hot brow on the cool glass. She brought it back and laid it on the glass again. Harder. Harder. On the fifth bang the glass splintered and her blood was running down the wall, down her face. The pain pierced her but the running blood seemed to let the worst of it out of her body. She poked out a splinter of mirror and looked at it through the film of blood. Then she put her palm on the wall in front of her and scraped the splinter across the back of her hand, welcoming the cleansing pain which streaked through her again.

She could not go back to the classroom now, because they would all see. She would just sit down and have a little rest and when the bleeding stopped and the pain stopped she would go home.

Twenty minutes into the lesson Miss Murray, her teacher, missed her and asked if anyone had seen Christine? Two of the girls exchanged glances. 'She was in the toilets Miss. We left her in the toilet. She was saying daft things.'

Later that day, Miss Murray stayed with Christine in the ambulance and in the hospital. She met the mother there, hauled by a telephone call from the shop where she worked. 'What happened, what happened?' Mrs. Cazelet said, taking Christine by her undamaged hand.

'There was an accident,' said Miss Murray. 'She fell against the mirror.'

'Fell? Fell?' Mrs. Cazelet bent down bringing her face close to her daughter's. Christine's bland eyes surveyed her from beneath the head bandage. 'Did you fall or were you pushed? Who did this to you?' said Mrs. Cazelet. 'I'll have them!'

Very slowly Christine shook her head. 'I can't tell. I'm not supposed to tell.'

Of course there was an enquiry. A policewoman even came to talk to Christine. But it was declared an accident and Miss Murray and Mrs. Cazelet heaved their respective sighs of relief and got on with things.

A month later, when her wounds were nicely healed,

Christine smashed the mirror again in the girl's toilets. This time she used her shoe on the very edge of the mirror. It was only the edge, so she could get a single splinter. This time she cut her arm above the cardigan line. She felt the mantle of relief thrown over her as the blood started to trickle. Then she pulled down her cardigan sleeves and went back to the classroom.

Twenty minutes later Miss Murray, patrolling the rows, saw the sticky trail of blood leading away from the exercise book in which Christine was writing. The trail led down the side of the desk into a pool on the floor.

This time Christine was bandaged up at a local surgery. Miss Murray went to the phone to tell her headmistress that there would be another accident form to fill in and that, really, she thought they should contact a social worker about Christine Cazelet. When she got back into the surgery Christine had gone. She ran to the door where she spotted the child making her way out of the surgery and along the road away from the school. She was too far away for her to shout, so Miss Murray followed her, walking briskly in her sensible low-heeled shoes.

Christine walked the few hundred yards to the edge of the town and along the cliff edge. Miss Murray's footsteps speeded up, and then slowed again as she saw Christine sit down at one of the seats which were placed on the cliffs for people to look out to sea to watch the waves and the tankers moving along the horizon.

Today the sea was a dense slate grey but there had been high winds and the breakers were smashing against the cliff, the spray leaping into the air and catching the light like silver fish.

Christine had been there a few minutes when,

puffing and breathless, Miss Murray plonked herself down. She spread her long, trunk-like legs before her. She smelled of mint and old cigarettes. 'Well now, Christine. I am at a loss. Why? Why do you do it?'

Christine glanced at her. 'I don't know, Miss.'

'Come on. You can't hurt yourself like that and not know why.'

'I don't know why, Miss.'

'Did you want a ride in the ambulance again?'

Christine shook her head.

'Did you want me to pay you some attention?'

The girl frowned up at her and shook her head. 'I wanted to hide it from you, Miss. Under my cardigan.'

There was a long silence, and then suddenly Miss Murray said, 'What did it feel like, when you did it?'

A vague smile crossed Christine's lips. 'Good. It felt OK.'

Christine was treated to more conversations after that, with the head teacher, with social workers and a man in an office who turned on a tape recorder and tapped his own hand a lot with his pencil. Christine's mother was defensive but genuinely bewildered. On three successive Saturday nights she couldn't face going out to dance. In all that time Christine did not hurt herself again. Even so she was as quiet as ever.

Then Mrs. Cazelet decided she was due for a night out and called on her nephew Seamus. Christine heard the call and went up to the bathroom and looked at herself in the mirror. She remembered the clanging sirens of the ambulance bell and Miss Murray's anxious face. She opened the door to the bathroom cabinet and took out one of her father's yellow disposable razors, and put it in her

31

cardigan pocket.

Then she went down, put on her padded jacket, thrust two bananas in the pocket and set out. She was four miles away when the found her that time. She was trudging along the cliff top, the hood of her jacket pulled up against the driving rain. In her pocket was the rotting peel of two bananas.

The third time Christine ran away she stole her father's lottery ticket money and caught a bus. This time she was twenty-five miles away when they caught up with her. Still, they didn't find the razor in her pocket.

Mrs. Cazelet admitted that Christine was quite beyond her control. 'You see this?' she said to the social worker. 'Look around you. A loving home. I work hard. Her dad works hard. Our Christine has everything she needs. What can I do?' She threw up her hands in genuine despair. 'Can you take her? For her own safety, only for her own safety? Perhaps for a little time. Till she realises she mustn't run…'

Christine Cazelet was taken into care because she couldn't make her mother listen to her.

Cut

Your skin holds you in
the shell of an egg
all neat inside. Embryo
and al-bu-men

Paulie Smith

6 DECENT BAGGAGE

Paulie: The buzzing cacophony of the street boils up around me. A woman bumps into me and I turn aggressively, reining in my prison-bred defences at the very last moment.

'Sorry,' she says. Just a harassed middle-class women about her business. Poor cow.

'Sorry,' I say. (Does she wonder who I am? This woman of twenty nine with a pasty face, wide staring eyes and two bursting carriers? Can you trust anyone without decent baggage?) Really I wouldn't blame her if she ran in terror.

I have to get off this street, crowded with this heaving, screaming mass of people, who dart about the pavement like mad hens with no one to control them. Some walk in groups and clusters, in ones and twos. I notice this woman not much older than me with a highly painted face. Clinging to her, arm-in-arm is a girl of fifteen or sixteen with long, flat hair. In her other hand are three glossy carriers with flashy designer markings.

Normally in prison they try to prepare you for this violent shock when you finally get out. They let you have practice runs: weekend leaves, where you can get used to being an ordinary person. But my own release pending appeal was different. It was almost instant. I shot onto these pavements like a bullet. The last time I was on a pavement was when they were bundling me into the paddy wagon with Queenie and the others. Bernie was there, of course, in the sneering crowd: right at the front row in his anorak and his Breton cap.

Today I crash through the double doors of the store and the place smells so sweet, like toffee apples drenched in cologne and cinnamon. The fluorescent light - clean, translucent as water - glances off the dazzling displays.

The girls behind the counters have rouge on their cheeks and very bright, painted eyes. I make my way to the lift and press button 10: Toys, Luggage and Accounts.

All the time - all the time – I keep looking behind me, waiting to be given permission by someone in uniform, for some blank face to nod or scowl at me and show me the right way. This is like treading very deep water, very far from the shore.

I walk slowly then stop to root around the shelves and find a black leather rucksack and a neat canvas hold-all. Decent baggage. The assistant at the till has clouds of doubt in her eyes; but she becomes bland and professional as I offer crisp, clean twenties in payment.

John Kebler, the psych, was in the prison this last Monday, asking me what I would need when I got out. All the signs were that I'd be out within the week, he said. He knew how quick this thing could be, how the world could hit you. He wanted to meet me at the gate when I got out. 'Let me know the time,' he said. His voice had the faintest of accents. German, probably, I thought. Maybe Swedish.

When I refused his offer, it was John Kebler who

suggested that the Gaia women should meet me at the gate. They did visit me the week before. They were great: crisp, female toughs edged with genuine sympathy. I liked them. But I turned them down. What I really wanted, I told John Kleber, was five hundred quid. He raised his eyebrows at this. 'They do say there'll be compensation.' I persisted. 'The Gaia solicitor said it would take time, but it will be there. A lot of money.' I said. 'So get them to advance me some of that.'

'It's a lot of money, Paulie, there is a danger…'

'There's no danger. Ask the Governor. I don't do drugs, or drink, do I? Never, even in here.'

He still hesitated. 'There is a process.'

'I'll pay you back twice,' I said. 'You can see the Governor and he'll fix it. They'll leave it in reception.'

There was a chit for the money. An officer took me to Reception to sign for it. She handed it over. It was on the list. Docketed. Signed by a deputy Governor in a sealed packet. The money was there. I was surprised. In fact, I didn't think John Kleber would come up with it.

Now, right here in the baggage department of this glossy store, I kneel down to transfer all my things from the carriers to the rucksack and tucked them in the holdall. The woman at the till shows an interest at last. 'I can't make up my mind whether you have been away, or you're going away,' she says, folding her arms.

I glance up at her. 'I've been away, love,' I say. 'And now I'm going on a journey.'

She meets my gaze and I have the sense of mutuality I've experienced a few times in prison, but never before. Never outside. The first time was with Queenie and Maritza and the others in the van. This really does happen from time to time, there in the ebb and flow of women in prison: it's an understanding without the need to say a word.

I stuff the carrier bags under the top flap of the hold-all and stand up. The woman nods at me, a ghost of a smile on her face. 'I hope your journey goes well.'

I look at her. 'It's down to me, I think.'

Apart from the taxi driver she is the first real person I have spoken to on the out. It feels good.

7 A SPOILT CHILD

Lilah: The mother ironed her daughter's hair between sheets of baking paper so that it fell like gleaming pump-water past her shoulders, nearly to her waist. Lilah's hair was her great success in life: always gleaming and smelling of fresh air, it was admired by the girls as well as the boys. The girls in school, then later her mates at the factory, took a kind of communal pride in Lilah's hair. The boys - she knew - dreamed of winding it around themselves as they kissed her, or fantasised on the way it might flow over the pillow right down to the floor as you looked at her from above.

In their dreams.

Lilah's favourite night was Friday. She worked as hard as anybody all week. Then came Friday night. Every Friday her mother made her a big plate of egg and chips. She got her dinner before the others, to give her plenty of time to get ready. Her mother made sure the water was hot, so she could have a long hot bath, soaking the dust of the factory out of her pores.

Lying there, breathing in scents that were already pervading the house, she could hear the others clattering in: the heavy tones of her brothers, the laughter of her sisters; the occasional groan or shriek of complaint, the thump of music, the vibrations flowing up through the bathroom floor.

They all knew she'd have had her tea early and would be upstairs soaking. Her sisters grumbled sometimes. 'You'd think no one else went out of this house on a Friday night.' But in the main they accepted her as queen of the castle. They were comfortable that she, the last one, the pretty one, should be the favourite. They accepted, too, that she should have the little car. It was safer, her being so young. She should not have to depend on lifts with all the risks that entailed.

Lilah's brothers and sisters were not too troubled by the fact that, indirectly, their pay packets contributed to her treats, her clothes, her car. In one way she was the child of them all. She was their surrogate. As a pretty child, ten years younger than her nearest sister, she'd been indulged from her first day. Everybody's pet. Never allowed to cry or to want, she had a sunny disposition and could cheer them all up with a flash of her perfect teeth and a toss of her long silky hair. They were all her slaves.

Three of her sisters and one of her brothers were married now and gone away from the house. But still there were four of them left, as well as her mother and father. Slaves and fans a-plenty, you might say.

The bathroom door rattled and Lilah's sister Maureen shouted through. 'Will you be in there all night? You're not the only one going out, lady.' But the tone was affectionate, not difficult to ignore. So Lilah relaxed and got out of the bath in her own time. Taking more fresh towels for her head and her shoulders, she stepped out of the bathroom, leaving a trail of soap, sponges and dripping water behind her on the landing.

In her bedroom she dried her hair, enjoying as

always the way it floated away from the nose of the dryer like rain from the wind. It felt clean and light, but sparkled and crackled, each strand fighting the next for air space. It needed her mother with the iron to settle it. That was the best thing, the iron.

It took two full applications to get her make-up right. What she most desired was to look as though she were wearing no make-up at all. The effect was glowing, starry, like she'd been lit up from the inside.

She pouted in the mirror and lowered her lashes. Then she laughed at herself and leapt into the skimpy, glittering top which showed her belly-button, the plain short black skirt and the black very high heels. The top and skirt were new, bought on the way home, and her high heels had been lovingly polished by her mother that afternoon by her mother. When she got down to the kitchen her brothers and sisters were spread around the house getting ready for their own Friday night. Her mother was sitting at the kitchen table reading the telly page in the evening paper. She looked at her daughter over the top of her glasses. 'You'll get your death of cold in that, Lilah. I tell you every time.' She did. It was her Friday night mantra.

Lilah laughed. 'I'll wear a jacket.' She would wear a jacket, but it would go straight into the boot of the car once she was away from the house. No one was seen dead in a jacket on a Friday night. 'There's just my hair,' she said. 'It's standing out like straw. Just look at it!'

Her mother put her glasses down on the paper and sighed.

'I'll do it myself,' said Lilah quickly. 'You sit down.'

'No. No. You'll singe it.' Her mother set up the

board and the iron, and got out the roll of baking paper from the kitchen drawer. Lilah pulled up a small wooden stool and sat on it, bare shiny knees nearly to her chin. Her mother took heavy hanks of hair, spread them out on the ironing board carefully protecting it with the baking paper and ironed them flat. She'd done this for ten years, since Lilah was seven: the action was as loving as a kiss.

The job over, Lilah stood up and shook her hair out, smoothing it with the small comb which she kept in the velvet bag whose narrow leather strap crossed her white shoulder and created an indentation between her small breasts.

Watching her, Lilah's mother sighed. 'You will watch your step out there, won't you?'

Lilah looked at her sideways through the silken curtain of hair. 'You know me, Mum. I'm always careful.'

'So, who are you going with?'

'Massa, Lynn and Joanna,' chanted Lilah. 'Who do I ever go with?'

Her mother nodded. These four girls had been inseparable since they started infant school. 'And the boys?' she asked. There were boys now.

'We'll meet them later on and maybe go on to Joanna's afterwards.'

'You won't …'

'I'll leave the car in the market place and get a taxi home.'

'It's a mistake, taking the car on Friday nights.'

Lilah shrugged. 'The girls expect it.' The other three girls lived in a village three miles distant. It was part of the iron-clad Friday routine that Lilah would pick them up and they should laugh all the way back into town before they had their great night out.

'Well, you watch yourself, lady' said Lilah's mother. 'Watch yourself.'

Lilah picked up her jacket. 'I've got my head screwed on. Don't you always say that, Mother?'

The pubs in the town had changed since Lilah first went into them. She'd been fifteen then. Then, it had been all lager, with boys - sometimes girls - spewing up on pavements. As the kids came out of the pubs there were always fights as one boy faced another down. Lilah and her friends kept clear of bother, although being on the very edge of the crowd gave them a buzz. There had been knifings and court cases but that made it all the more edgy, more exciting. And lads they'd been at school with ending up behind bars!

That buzz in the crowd still attracted them, but now there was Ecstasy, which made you love the world. It calmed down some sections of the crowd, kept the rest dancing longer. Ecstasy was common. There was a bit of coke about as well, but that was hard to get, at first. Some of the boys would go into the city to get supplies. The coke made Lilah uneasy. She would have nothing to do with it. She turned down offers of E as well. She said she could make herself high and couldn't she dance all night anyway? She could outlast the lot of them.

Still, there was a bigger edge to things these days, an edgy-precipice feeling, a train-roaring-down-the-track feeling. Now, instead of dancing the night away together, with occasional time out for a bit of snogging with some handy lad, the four girls had linked up with four special lads. Lilah got the pick: Jonno, whose dad had taxis and who always had a pocket full of cash.   The others paired off. Joanna drew the short straw and had to put up with Alan Newton who was short and sniffed a lot.

But the girls still had their own good time, their own laughs before the boys joined them at ten.   After that, they all danced together, unable to talk because of the noise. Jonno's friend Mal, who'd paired off with Lynn, always had a pocketful of Es. Lilah watched the others after they'd done the Es, enjoying their embraces and dancing alongside them into the night. But she stayed clear of actually taking anything.

Tonight was no different from any other. The laughs and the lager. Their final pub, The Sentinel, was as crowded as ever; now and then the DJ did cartwheels on his tiny podium.   They were all dancing. Joanna was even draped around Alan Newton as though he were something special.

Mal's hand came under her nose. 'Fancy one, Lilah? Get one down your neck. You're getting as miserable as hell these days. Isn't she Lynn?'

Lynn, who was hanging onto Mal's arm, laughed out loud. 'Get one, Lilah. Put some love into yer.'

Lilah shook her head, laughing always longer and louder than the rest. 'Nah! Don't need it.' She shouted above the beat. 'Don't need it.'

Jonno whispered in her ear. 'Get one, kid. How d'you know what you need?' His hand grasped her arm very tight. 'Proper bloody killjoy you are. Get one, will you?'

'Try a half,' Lynn yelled, looking at her, cool, serious now. 'Go on, Lilah, try a half and stop being a baby.'

Lilah shrugged. 'Oh, well…' So they cheered her, cheered her on.

Jonno paid Mal the money then took the half and laid it on the palm of his gleaming hand, like a rider offering a sugar lump to a horse. 'There now, Lilah. Don't I spoil you?'

Lilah had been right. The tablets didn't really affect her. She just danced a bit more, laughed a bit more; her natural delight in the world was enhanced. The tablets didn't affect her. She drank her water. She never panicked. In the end she could do six or seven half tablets in one night and all they did was make the party swing in a better direction.

8 CAFETERIA

Paulie At last, with this decent baggage I know I don't stand out too much in the city crowd. It's easy to progress from the store to Gap to buy jeans and sweaters, to Robinson's to buy sturdy shoes which are nearly boots and to Boots to buy the absolute essentials for the face. All the time I'm relishing the delight of moving freely from counter to counter, through doorway after doorway without asking anyone's permission.

I make my way back to the store and into the Lady's Room to change into my new gear and to ram my old stuff into the carrier bags then into the refuse bin. I make a call on the public phone near the lingerie department. Then on up to the cafeteria to have tea in a hand-thrown pottery cup, and a squashy cream cake on a thick matching plate. I even have a steel fork with which to eat my cake. That's new. Young Christine would have had a field day with that fork, on the inside. What patterns on her arm! *The marks on my arms ain't nothing to the marks inside.'* She once said that to me.

I'm onto my second gorgeous cake when John Kebler strides into the café, flustered and looking out of place among the shoppers. He's smoother and heavier than when I first met him. And now he's wearing rimless glasses that hide his thick lashes. He's moved up the professional ladder now and is rarely, rather than routinely, at the prison. He's a full professor at the University, and is quoted in the papers and on TV about aspects of the confinement of women. He's been on TV a few times in recent weeks, responding to questions about my own case. He's very articulate on all that and I'm pleased to say doesn't tell lies to save his or anybody else's bacon.

Now he shakes my hand briskly and surveys me from head to toe. 'You look good, Paulie,' he says. 'Hard to think you've been out just a few hours.'

'I suppose you thought I'd be a jittery wreck.' I look him up and down. 'You don't look so bad yourself, John. Academic life definitely suits you.'

He flushes slightly at this. Then takes refuge in ordering tea from the hovering waitress. Then he says. 'You always could wrong-foot me, Paulie. You've done that from the first time we met.'

'I do have this problem with status,' I say.

'And what's that?'

'I can't recognise it.'

'Well, you must have had a hard time in prison, then.' He smiles, easy now.

I hunch my shoulders. 'Not a bit. Prison's not about status. It's about rules and power. You just have to handle yourself in the middle of all that. To teach yourself to know how it works.'

'That reminds me.' He reaches into his inside pocket and pulls out a slim pale green volume. It has my name on its cover and the strap line says *Containment*. It's well-thumbed. 'Thank you for sending me this. Will you sign it for me?'

I sign it with my special translucent green fountain pen.

The waitress comes with his tea and he pours himself a cup.

'Your book's very good,' he offers. 'I've used it a lot.'

'Used it?' My brows climb up into my hair. '*Used* it?

'Referred to it.' His brown cheeks stain pink, 'I've quoted it in seminars. In so-called learned articles.'

'Mmm,' I say, twisting my mouth. So-called.'

'Does that offend you?' He leans forward. 'I wouldn't want to step on your toes.'

I have to laugh out loud at this. 'Stop peering at me with those forensic eyes. A normal poet - a poet on the out - would you have asked her permission? Would you have communicated with her about your intentions before you did it?'

'Yes ... No... I don't know. Yes of course I would.' He is red faces, blustering. 'I just know that everyone is astonished at the quality -the insight. They're surprised how someone inside could have written such stuff.'

'Like how can a monkey actually paint?'

'No. You know it's not like that, Paulie.' He paused, taking a sip of his tea. 'It's really authentic. Good stuff.'

'If there's any good stuff there, it's all down to Queenie. And Stewart Pardoe.'

'Queenie?' he says. 'Down to Queenie?'

9 SOUP KITCHEN

Queenie: 'There we are, Queenie!' The pale faced girl smiled brightly as she ladled soup into the mug clasped in the old woman's faintly grimy hands. 'And there is bread at the end of the table, look.'

'Thank you. Kind of you, dear.'

The helper - a pale, kind girl who was volunteering in the soup kitchen for a month before she went off to help build a school in Africa - watched the old woman waddle away to her accustomed place at the end of the table. Old woman? You never knew how old these people were, in the soup kitchen.

Maud, the brisk woman who had set up this soup kitchen, told her on her first day, 'Decide how old they look, dear, then take off twenty years.' That should make this old bird no more than sixty-five. Shame. The girl smiled brightly at her next customer, a man who by Maud's formula must be no more than thirty.

Queenie relished the soup and the thick, substantial bread. She had to dip the bread in the soup these days, due to trouble she was having with two of her teeth on the left side. These were terribly painful, so much so today that there were thick knuckles of bread which she couldn't tackle, hungry as she was.

'Not want those, missis?' The young man who had followed her in the queue was sitting opposite her, slurping his soup. He nodded to her rejected bread.

'No. No. Can't manage it. Teeth, you know!'

'Givin' you gyp, are they?'

Queenie's pushed the hard lumps towards the young man and let her gaze wander away over his shoulder. She always needed to keep an eye on her bags, stacked carefully in the corner. She'd had her bags stolen once by some ne-er-do-well and that had caused her real heartache. She'd had to go into a shelter for a week and they started to give her those pills again, those pricks with needles. So she'd run off again, taking a couple of their own Sainsbury carriers, stuffed with a few things that were lying around. You never knew when they'd come in useful. A brush. A bottle of ink. Some pillowcases. Two old cardigans. Some climbing socks. She looked longingly into the bottom of her cup.

'More soup?' The kind girl was beside her, holding a white enamel jug in her hand, like a Greek maiden on a vase.

Queenie nodded and held up her cup like a child.

'And was there something wrong with the bread?' The girl frowned at the young man who was chewing away at Queenie's tough crusts.

'She give it to us,' he said defensively. 'She give it to me seeing as her teeth are giving her gyp.'

Queenie nodded. 'Back left,' she said briefly. 'Don't know how it's happened dear. I always had perfect teeth you know. My father had his own teeth till he died, you know. Lived till the age of eighty-nine. Born when Victoria was on the throne.' She slurped the soup. 'But then, he knew teeth.'

'Did he?' said the girl. 'How did he know teeth?'

Queenie nodded. 'Dentist,' she said.

'A dentist?' The girl's glance became brighter, spotting an opportunity 'There's a dentist who comes here, Queenie. Calls here on Thursdays. He'll have a look at them. At your teeth. He'll stop them hurting.'

Queenie placed her cup on the stained bench and shook her head. 'No thank you dear. That is very good of you but the danger is they'll take me inside. Lock me up, like they did when I lost my bags. Pumping you full of rubbish.'

'Liquid coshes. That's what they use', said the young man. 'They use them in jail as well. Ask anybody. Any more soup for me?' He put his mug under the girl's nose, holding it very still while she filled it to the brim.

'That's very well named.' said Queenie. 'Liquid cosh. Dulls you down so you can't live any more, or see things.' She paused. 'Things you want to see, that is.'

'No! No, Queenie,' said the girl eagerly. 'It's not like that. They don't want you to …'

Queenie tied her third scarf around her neck, and her second scarf round the back of her old hat. She fixed the girl with a look that in the old days had frozen many a child in Junior Three. 'Well, dear, you weren't there, were you?'

'Look!' said the girl desperately, 'They just take a look at you here, in that room back there. Then they can give you something to take the pain away. If you need any more than that, they can take you off to the surgery there and then, or make an appointment…'

'Surgery,' said Queenie, shaking her head.

'Whisky,' said the man. 'That's the best thing for toothache. They should give you whisky.'

The girl looked from one derelict to the other. It wasn't that you wanted gratitude. Sometimes all you wanted them to do was listen to you. She turned away, and then turned back. 'Thursdays,' she said. 'This dentist comes on Thursdays, Queenie, between ten and eleven.'

'Whisky,' said the man. 'That's best.'

Queenie stood up and poked around inside her bags, checking the items to make sure nobody had stolen them while she was talking to that pushy girl. They taught them nothing nowadays. No restraint. No manners. She was pleased she'd had no children. Nothing but trouble. Children.

When Thursday came round Queenie had quite forgotten the conversation with the girl. So she was surprised when the girl brought a young man in a red anorak to her end of the table.

'Queenie,' she said brightly. 'This is Jimmy O'Brien. He's a dentist and he could help you with that aching tooth of yours.'

'Dentist?' She surveyed him from head to toe. 'He's not a dentist.'

The young man smiled an enameled white smile. 'Now, what makes you say that, Queenie?'

'Well, first, you're dressed like a ploughman, and second if you were a dentist you would call me by my correct name. A professional man would have manners.'

He slid onto the bench beside her. 'So what is your correct name?' She could smell a sickly smell of violets, overlaid by something very like *Rive Gauche,* in fact. Men smelling like women! A queer state of things. She moved to the very edge of the bench. 'Miss Pickering,' she said.

'Miss Pickering? Well, Miss Pickering,' he surveyed his smooth fingers, his perfectly manicured nails. 'All I am asking is that we go over into that little room there and you let me take a look-see. Is it hurting now?'

'Yes,' she said reluctantly. 'Like that chap over there said the other day. It's giving me gyp. Especially at night. With the cold.'

The dentist and the girl exchanged glances. Nights under bridges or in shop doorways would certainly make one's teeth ache.

The girl coughed. 'Queenie ... Miss Pickering ... was telling me her father was a dentist, Jimmy.'

'Is that so? Well, Miss Pickering, he'd have told you that they shouldn't be neglected. Teeth.'

Queenie stirred in her seat and frowned at him 'Well. No harm in letting you take a look-see, I suppose.' *Take a look-see*! She hadn't heard that for many years. She had never even said it herself. Her father used to jolly up his patients with that phrase.

The other two exchanged glances.

'I wouldn't have gone to him,' Queenie announced suddenly.

'Who?'

'My father.'

'Why not?' The young dentist was interested.

'He was never happier than taking the whole lot out – every single tooth - and planting in a false set. He had a tidy mind, do you see? But it wasn't fair. Not fair at all. Some very good teeth went into his bin. Some very fine teeth. My mother's teeth, for instance. They went in his bin too. The lot. She never forgave him! He made her into an old woman in a morning.'

A frown marred the smooth brow of Jimmy O'Brien. 'I know they did do that at one. Time. The theory was that decaying teeth harboured disease. They were mistaken, Miss Pickering. It would never be allowed now.'

'He knew better than that. Just look at him, my father. Died in his eighties with a mouthful of teeth. Only three extractions in his life. Not fair.' She paused. '*Mrs. Do-As-You-Would-Be-Done-By*!' she said suddenly.

'What?' Now he was entirely lost.

'She's in *The Water Babies* by Charles Kingsley. The children in my class loved that story. *Mrs. Do-As-You-Would-Be-Done-By*. Do you see? If my father pulled out all their teeth he should have had that done to him. D'you see?'

'Well, Miss Pickering. I promise you we never take them all out now. We move heaven and earth to keep what's there, right in your mouth. I promise.'

Queenie got up, and reached for her bags. 'Very well young man. You can take a *look-see*.' And then, she fixed him with a severe glance. 'We'll see if you really do know your job.'

In the little room there was a dentist's chair of the more portable kind. Jimmy O'Brien pulled on his rubber gloves and fixed a disposable bib over Miss Pickering's scarves. He talked to her all the time, worrying that if there were a gap in the talk. That this one would fly away from under his hand like a captured bird. He asked her to open wide and took a look at her mouth, this way, that way. His hands were gentle. Then he stood back. 'Look, Miss Pickering, would you like to get this over with now?'

'Over?' It was a problem, from her prone position, keeping her eye on her bags, which the girl had put in the corner.

'There are two teeth in here that look a bit of a … look a bit poorly and do need extracting. There is one other that we might manage to save. If you come with me now…'

'Come with you?' She sat up straight, noting that her bags were still safe. 'Come with you? You might be Jack the Ripper. They said he was really a dentist.' She bustled past the girl and retrieved her bags. 'Or was it a doctor?'

'Janette here will come with us. You know Janette, don't you?'

'She has to give out the soup. She has a job.'

'They've let her off. So she can help you.'

Queenie pulled her hat down hard. 'Very kind of them I'm sure.'

'Will you come?' For the first time there was an edge to his voice. 'Will you come, for your own sake?'

She shrugged. 'Well, dear, if it means so much to you. But make sure my bags are safe.'

After the young dentist had extracted the teeth her face felt odd, as though only her eyes and her nose belonged to her and beneath them was a great yawning gap. And she was slavering! She only realised that when the slaver dropped on her coat. She couldn't even feel herself slavering. What were things coming to? Then, one by one she smoothed out her scarves and tied them round her neck in the special way she had. The girl tried to help; tried to place her hat on her head. Queenie shook off the girl's hand. 'I can manage dear.' It was all very strange but it was good to be without the terrible pain.

'Now what shall we do with you?' said the girl called Janette, a bright, satisfied smile on her face.

'What shall you do with me? You? With me?' But she had to mumble the furious words. She herself could not even understand what she said. How shameful.

Janette and the dentist exchanged glances. 'Now, Miss Pickering,' said the dentist, taking off his rubber gloves. 'You need to be very careful, just for a little time. A day, two at the most. Just so no cold gets into that jaw. Just till that local wears off. So we have a bed in the ward near here…'

She mumbled again. 'No. No bed.'

'I know you don't like it, but I promise, promise, you that you'll be out in a day, two at the most.'

Promises! Piecrusts! She looked at the earnest young face above her. The child meant it. She knew that. The boy meant to be kind. But he didn't realise. He didn't know what they did with you, once they got you in there. They took your bags away and put them in the incinerator. They inveigled you into a bath. They couldn't wait to wash the smells of the street out of your hair. Then they got out their rattling bottles.

Still, Queenie meekly allowed Janette to settle her comfortably in the waiting room while she went off to sign some forms or other for the dentist. Then Queenie stood up and crept, with only the barest rustle of her bags, out of the room, out of the place. She has run away down one of her favourite and familiar back streets before the ink was dry on the dentist's for

10 SLIM VOLUME

Paulie: 'Queenie?' John Kebler is looking at me frowning

I tell John Kebler the story of the long nights in the cell, and the poetry that Queenie chanted to me. And how she told me to write poems and how it didn't matter if they didn't actually rhyme. How she said that it was about the song and the rhythm in the words. I told him of the poems she chanted to me, the poems she had off by heart. They all rhymed and had the rhythm of a metronome.

John Kebler knows about the prison writer Stewart Pardoe, of course. That was public knowledge. Their paths had crossed quite often as they busied about their quasi-official roles in prison. Neither officer not teachers, they saw a lot in prison.

Stewart Pardoe was quite famous but he didn't look it. He was this old guy, who had never realised the sixties had ended. He wore a Stetson hat and his original cowboy jacket with the flowers embroidered on it. Would be worth a lot on those vintage shops now. He came to my prison when I was on the third year of my sentence and he ran these ace poetry workshops for three months. Women went to the workshops just because it was something to do. But I was mad keen. Truth to tell, encouraged by Queenie in those early weeks I'd been scribbling really raw stuff almost from the beginning of my sentence.

In those sessions and the days in between I read

Stewart's own poems and reams of other stuff he put my way - Sylvia Plath, Seamus Heaney, W.B.Yeats, Ted Hughes, Emily Dickinson, and Carol Ann Duffy. So many.

At first I thought the language, as it lay dead there on the page, looked ordinary, mundane, even empty. Then I realized that spoken into the air they made more sense. Then during those long prison nights the images and the ideas, the rhythms and the meaning jumped up at me from the pages and began to echo and re-echo in my mind. They began to join forces in my head with all that Browning and Keats that Queenie chanted to me in those early prison days after we arrived together in the white van. Soon, lines from my own life were joining up in my head like iron filings on a paper responding to a magnet.

I showed Stewart some of the poems I'd been writing. He was kind but I knew he thought them half-baked affairs, naïve in the extreme. But he took time to read and think about them and he pulled me on. He started tightening me up like a screw, till my own stuff had more compression about it, more energy. But I never kidded myself that the stuff was really good. I'd have had to be deluded to think like that.

It was Stewart, before he died, who got money from somewhere to publish my collection in the slim volume. Official Home Office permission had to be granted, of course. There was some enthusiasm for the book on the out, but there's no way of knowing that this was not intellectual philanthropy or a guilty kindness on behalf of some sensitive liberal minded people. Despite some plaudits I've always wondered whether the excitement was tinged with the frisson that comes from seeing monkeys paint those awful daubs.

'It's the books I want to talk to you about,' I say now to John in Fenwick's cafeteria.

'You want to write another collection? Have you material?'

I shake my head. 'No. Not now. Perhaps not ever. But look.' I open the battered flyleaf of his copy at the printed dedication. *To Queenie, Christine, Maritza and Lilah, with love and gratitude.*'

'I have a pile of the books with me. These women were all gone by the time Stewart came to my jail. What I want to do is to take the books to them. To give them their own copy. I asked about this on the inside, whether I could get their addresses to send them their own copy. But they were baffled, of course. Resistant. You know the ethos. Everything is either impossible or not possible at all.'

He laughs. 'So you say, Paulie.'

Now I begin wonder just how old John Kleber is. Forty? Fifty? He has very nice hands. Not too large. Well shaped. No, don't worry. I'm not falling into the trap of falling for my psych. Transference? I've read all about it, of course. I'm way past that. 'Anyway,' I say to him firmly. 'As a very last favour, I want you to pull rank, use contacts, to let me know where I can find Queenie and the others.'

'Will you post the books to them?'

'No. I want to take them to them. I want to see them. I haven't seen them since those first months on remand.'

'Why so keen? That was a long time ago, Paulie. You seem inordinately keen. Why is it so important?'

'The truth is, I don't know. Ever since I knew I was coming out, those four women have been bobbing away in my mind again. I'd locked them away somewhere in the last year or two. But in these last weeks as I realised I would be free there they were, bobbing in front of me. I've dreamed about Queenie twice. In one dream we were buying her a new hat. In another she was drowning and I was trying in vain to save her. Another time in a dream I glimpsed Maritza and Christine: an unlikely pairing - one so neat, the other so large and ungainly. And through the years every time I saw a young woman come into prison more or less destroyed by drugs, I thought of Lilah.'

I stop talking but he still stays silent, leaving me space to say what I want to say.

'Perhaps in those early weeks, for me - this person who'd barely had any family – for me, these women became my family. So soon found, so soon lost.'

John Kebler holds up the teapot. 'Would you like a cup of my tea? Or shall I get you a new pot?'

11 MY NAME IS CHRISTINE

Christine: At the residential school Christine Cazelet came up against Phoebe Bliss, known to everyone as Tigger. Compared with Christine's tall bony bulk, Tigger was tiny: small face, small feet, something like a marmoset. Her fingers were very short, giving her hands the appearance of paws. She had a very wide mouth and a very foul vocabulary, which Christine soon learned to share.

After one or two wrestling fights, (which Christine finally let Tigger win), they became best friends. Their friendship involved dodging about together a bit, playing snooker with the boys and mostly beating them. It involved telling really weird ghost stories in the dark. It involved sharing and exchanging clothes, although this was not always easy because of the difference in their sizes. It also involved recognizing that the rest of the world was really their enemy.

The two girls regularly patrolled the ragged beauty of the two acre garden attached to the house, which had once been the home of a well-to-do shipbuilder, then a hospital for the wounded from the Great War, then a private boarding school before its present incarnation as a school to contain children who seemed otherwise uncontainable. Christine and Tigger climbed trees and smoked skinny spliffs and stolen cigarettes. The very long, very high stone had once kept poachers out, now did good service keeping recalcitrant children in.

The girls didn't speak with each other about why they were there in that place. In fact Christine didn't know, quite, why she was there. After her mother finally washed her hands of her, Social Services had placed her with a foster family in a sprawling house on the edge of town. There were two other foster children in the house - yet more flotsam and jetsam beached up in the care system. Flora and Jenny, the other two girls, were thrilled to be there, so busy playing good children and mummies and daddies that Christine wanted to vomit.

'We only have two rules here, Chris …' she was told by Jo, the solid, foster mum who knew her stuff.

'Christine,' said Christine, her glance sliding round Jo to take in the fish tank that was built into the wall, 'that's my name.'

'Well Christine, we only have two rules here.' said Jo. 'One is that you turn up for tea at six o'clock. The other is you always let me know where you are. There's a mobile phone there for you. Oh! And everyone does one job off the list every day.' She nodded at the extensive list stuck to the fridge. This list covered every household task from mopping the hall floor to cleaning the taps. 'Oh, and if you just tick them we'll know the job's done. No good doing a job twice, is there?' She beamed, showing her large, perfectly formed teeth which stuck out very slightly.

'That's three,' said Christine.

'What?' said Jo.

'Three rules.' Christine put her head down and wouldn't meet Jo's gaze.

In the management of her foster home, Jo had her own very powerful secret weapon. This appeared on the table every day at six o'clock. She was a stupendous cook. Perfect pies, perfect burgers, perfect succulent chips, mashed potatoes soft as snow, chops tender as jelly. The array was endless. She was just as good at sweets: lemon meringue pie, trifle, fruit salad…

The other two kids, Fiona and Jenny, glugged all this up and felt well and truly fostered. Christine ended up thinking that Jo just fostered children to have a regular and appreciative audience for her culinary skills. Still, Christine herself glugged alongside the others. In the four months she survived at Jo's she put on nearly a stone in weight. Her face rounded, her limbs rounded and, most horrible of all, her breasts rounded.

In Jo's house Christine felt stranded on Mars, on Jupiter, the other side of the sun. Sometimes she saw all their mouths opening and closing and couldn't hear what they were saying. Jo's husband, Max, was quieter than Jo, his coming and going from his job at the council was an automatic part of the household, like the whirring of the washer and the tea on the table at six o'clock. The day he looked over his paper and winked at Christine, her heart went into spasm. She stopped eating her tea, fled upstairs and locked her door. Jo came up after half an hour and, after pleading to be let in banged hard on the door. 'Let me in, Chris.'

'Christine,' roared Christine.

'Let me in. This is stupid. You know this is stupid. There is perfectly good food wasting down there.'

'Food. Food. Greedy pigs,' chanted Christine. 'Food, food, greedy pigs.'

Then Jo battered harder on the door and Christine could hear the lower tones of Max's voice. She scrabbled under her bed for her case and pulled back the lining to get at the razor she had taken all those months ago from her mother's bathroom cabinet.

It was so easy. The benediction of sharp sensation and the flood of pain, then the dull throb of feeling and the healing pulse of blood. She waited until she was calm and went to pull back the door. Then she backed off and dropped onto the bed.

Jo grabbed a towel from the radiator and darted forward. 'Chris, what have you done? What have you done?'

Christine looked at her, eyes wide and empty. 'Christine,' she said wearily. 'My name is Christine.'

After an overnight at the hospital she wouldn't go back with Jo and Max. 'The food's bloody awful,' she said as the social worker bundled her into her car.

'But Jo's food is lovely. Flora and Jenny love it.'

'They're greedy pigs,' said Christine. 'I want to go home to my Mum. You tell her I'll be a good girl. A good girl, if she'll let me come home.'

But her mother, hearing of the new episode, couldn't face having her. After that, Christine was placed in another foster place, from which she ran away back to her mother's home and barricaded herself in the bathroom. This time her mother sent for the social worker, who brought a female police officer with her. The two of them broke down the door. When they got into the tiny room Christine was sitting on the edge of the bath glaring at them. They looked round for blood and there was none. The room was shining bright, clean as always.

The social worker reached out for her and Christine flung out her arm against the woman, making her lose her balance and fall awkwardly between the toilet and the bath.

'Chris…' The police officer stepped over the social worker and took her by the shoulders. Christine kicked her on the shin and she swore, but held on tight.

In the end they hauled her, kicking and screaming, down the stairs and out of the door. All along the street the curtains twitched. They were pulled back further when the watchers saw the child being pushed into the social worker's car and then dodging straight out of the opposite door. Their curtains were opened wider when the child ran along the road, pursued by both the police officer and the social worker, to be hauled back and placed - successfully this time - in the police car.

The social worker climbed in beside her and held both her hands. 'Chris… Chris… This is no good. No good at all.'

Christine looked her in the eyes. 'You can let me go now. I won't run. And Christine. Christine is my name.'

That, she supposed, must be the reason why she ended in the big house with the tall, locked gates. But at least here she'd got to know Tigger. So it wasn't all bad. But this was a very secure place and some of the kids in there had done very bad things like stealing knives and hurting animals, even people.

In some ways this place was better than Jo's house, because it was not so personal. You were not so much an audience for someone else's virtue. Here you had to make your bed, keep your things tidy, turn up for meals. But these meals were crap-awful so you didn't have to be grateful. You turned up for lessons. These involved easy tasks - filling in messy moth-eaten workbooks - so that wasn't too bad.

They did *Art* on Fridays and, though she didn't show it, Christine thought that was OK. The bloke that did it didn't bother you too much. He put nice paints and pastels out for you and showed you how he did it. Then you messed about and did your own version.

She wrote dozens of letters to her mother, apologising, apologising for all the trouble she'd made and saying that she'd never, never do any of that again. She watched the post and after two weeks, when nothing came back, she broke a mirror and cut herself in the laundry, splashing blood over the clean sheets.

But in this place there was no panic. Here, they were geared for this kind of thing. The doctor stitched and bandaged her in the pristine surgery and tried to talk to her about why she did it. 'Drawing attention to yourself in this way will only harm you, Christine,' she said, putting her scissors back in the locked cabinet.

Christine frowned. 'Attention?'

'Why do you do it?'

She looked into the eyes of this woman. They were kind enough. 'It helps,' she said. 'It helps me.'

Christine never got home for weekends but some of the kids coming back off weekend leave smuggled bottles of booze into the house. It could be anything. Beer. Wine. Martini was a favourite as it hit you faster. It was mostly boys who brought it in but the girls could get their hands on their stuff easily enough, in return for favours.

Christine was not one for favours. She would not let the boys come near her. After one or two scraps they didn't bother her. She was bigger and stronger than most of them: handy with her feet and her fists. It was Tigger who let them put their hands up her blouse and down her skirt, earning her the paper cups of booze which she shared with Christine. One day she vanished altogether for half an hour with one of the boys and came back into the room to produce, with the flourish of a magician, a whole bottle of whisky from under her scrap of a cardigan, .

They waited until after supper and retired to Chritine's room where they turned their radio right up. They danced and drank the whisky very fast, finally falling on the bed in a stupor, the radio still blaring. The night staff who came to tell them to turn off their radio saw the empty bottle and the state the two girls were in and caused a ruckus. He gave them some bitter water to drink which made them sick, then made them drink litres of water. Then he stood over them in their bedrooms while they stripped their beds and remade them with fresh sheets. Then he stood over them in the vast laundry while they bundled their sheets into one of the washers and turned it on.

Finally he watched them into bed and turned off the light. 'I'll talk to you in the morning. The first thing you will do is tell me where you got that stuff.'

But they never did.

Christine wrote to her mother again. This time she swore that Seamus had really been all right. That he had never hurt her. That she had been making it all up. She would come home and show her Mum how good she could be. If only her Mum would forgive her.

This time a new social worker brought the letter back to her unopened. 'I know it's hard, Chris, but your Mum's not been too well lately. She can't take all this pressure. Just leave off these letters for six months or so.

Can you do that?'

'My name is Christine,' she growled. 'Christine.'

The woman's shoulders went up. 'No need to be like that Christine. How was I to know?'

That night, when Christine cut herself, she carved fine lines right down her forearms to the backs of her hands. It made a regular pattern. Straight lines, separated from each other but leading to the same place.

It took a lot of concentration to do the whole arm but she did and in the maze of pain there was some relief. It was Tigger who found her and went screaming for help. It was Tigger who cried. No-one had ever cried for her before.

It was hospital this time, swirling lights, screaming siren, the lot. Tigger had wanted to get in the ambulance with her but they had held her back. In a woozy state, Christine was hurting like hell now the blood flow had stopped. The last thing Christine saw was Tigger's anxious little monkey face, wet with tears.

12 A KISS ON THE CHEEK

Paulie: 'To be honest I don't know why I want to take the books to them, to put them in their hands,' I say now to John Kebler. 'I just need to see those women. How they are. You know.'

He suddenly sits up straight, glances at his watch. 'I'm sorry, Paulie. I dashed out of a meeting to get here. I have to get away.'

'Yeah. Yeah. You go off. I've all the time in the world.'

'You have somewhere to stay?'

I shake my head. 'I'll find somewhere.'

He pauses. 'You could stay at my house.'

I have to laugh at this. How many rules is he breaking here? 'Nah. Your wife wouldn't like that. Getting mixed up with prisoners on the out. Bad move. And you know you're not supposed to.'

He stares hard at me. 'Think about it Paulie. You're not a prisoner, you're not an arsonist. You're a poet. A poet!'

'Stewart would take issue with you there. And your wife'd not look kindly on me coming. She would be mad if she did. I know it. I would be.'

He smiles a new smile, a personal smile. Somehow

67

it freezes me to the marrow. 'You're probably right Paulie. You're just a bit too good looking to be a non-threatening guest. Even for a poet.' He fishes out a card. 'But there's my home number. Keep in touch in the next week or two and I'll see what I can do about the whereabouts of those women. Should be impossible. But I'll see.'

He stands up to go and I stand up with him. He leans across and kisses my cheek, as though he were my friend. 'Make a go of it, Paulie,' he says. 'Make a go of it and we'll all be grateful to feel less guilty.' He paused. 'I can never quite deal with the fact that my report was no help all those years ago. That my inadequacy was part of the trap which was sprung on you.'

This makes me smile. 'So you yourself have counseling for that, do you?'

'You bet I do,' he said.

As he weaves his way through the busy, bright places and the clattering tables and chairs I sit back down and touch my face where he has kissed me. That's the first kiss I've had since the very early days in the squat, when Charlie kissed me, when he was still my golden boy. I've had lots of chances since, but that's not my fancy. I've seen some very tender relationships between women inside, sometimes very passionate. At times I have been jealous, feeling the arid desert of neutrality around me like a fence. I respected the comfort these women could offer each other but, like I say, women were never my fancy.

13 SPIDER'S WEB

About Paulie: When she was young Paulie Smith had been very well aware that they suspected her of setting fire to her father.   Through the months, then the years, of gentle questioning, the cunning adult ploys pressed on and on making her feel almost impelled to say yes, yes! She'd done it. Yes, like they said, she was desperate about the way she'd had to live with him.   Yes, she did pour vodka over her father and put a match to him.   It would have been a relief to say it, to agree, to agree with them.   But she knew the truth and drew back from agreeing with them and knew they were angry even when they smiled.

The police, then the social workers, had been very intrigued at the array of goods in the pantry in the house where she and her father lived. They recognised the squirrel hoard of a compulsive thief.   Well, that was something to get through to her. They questioned her as a thief as well as that other, worse, thing.   Even so, in the circumstances, charges were not pressed.   There was the issue of the fire, though, even if she hadn't wanted to be rid of her father. Did she like to light fires?   They so wanted to get her into some kind of pigeonhole. Thief! Fire-raiser!   Young as she was, she saw that they loved labels.   But she admitted nothing.   If you did that yourself there was no hope, was there?

Still, she had been quite well looked after.   She had her own social worker, a sympathetic woman from

WENDY ROBERTSON

Haverford West; she even had her own counsellor for a
year or so. After all, this motherless girl had lost her father
and had every right to be traumatised. With the woman
from Haverford West, despite the gentlest of probing, the
slickest of enabling, Paulie still wouldn't admit that her
father had abused her. She would shake her head at that.
'No. He was too sad at first. Too drunk at the end.'
Anyway, did the woman not realize that he'd loved her
mother with such great passion? That was the problem,
wasn't it? He was just very sad. The woman sighed
restlessly, denied the looked-for disclosure for which her
training had trained her.

After the inquest Social Services found Paulie good
digs so she could stay on for the Sixth Form. She went back
to her old school, where she was forgiven all old trespasses
as she was now a Deserving Case. She had good exam
results. Her teachers gave her references which got her a
place at an ex Polytechnic. The references must have been
very partial, because she was turned down by three older
universities and one other ex-polytechnic before this place
was secured.

At college she lived in digs and worked very hard.
She stopped shoplifting because now that was not
necessary as it had been when she was taking care of her
father; her plight raised sympathy and secured her decent
funding. And she'd stopped using *Es* because now they
brought no joy - just visions of her father in flames.
Sometimes she had visions of both her father and mother
in flames.

She lay low during her teaching course, got good
grades and was seen as quiet but efficient as she played at
being a teacher in the classroom. On teaching practice she

conformed to the school dress code - hair cut to a bob. short skirts, high neck. She even found her leisure-time style was dulling down to safe clothes that would 'do in school'. Her resources were limited, so it meant these clothes or nothing. Once or twice, in a big store in town, it crossed her mind that she might have grafted stuff again, but something stopped her. She wanted no more gentle probing: No more help.

Paulie's first teaching job was in a small industrial town in the North and it was on her train journey that she met the man who wanted conversation, whose name, he told her, was Bernie Cooper. That night it was in Bernie Cooper's house she slept, fully clothed with a chair jammed under the door handle.

The next morning, Paulie sat bolt upright. Someone was rattling the door off its hinges. 'Are you gonna stay there all day?' a male voice hollered. 'It's eight o'clock. You'll lose that fuckin' job of yours, I'm tellin' yer.'

She lay still and listened to his feet padding down the steps. Then she poked her head out of the door, dashed to the bathroom, stripped off for a wash and pulled on clean, crumpled clothes from her case. That headmistress would have to like that or lump it. She'd been smart enough at the interview, and she'd explain that she had just arrived and was looking for digs.

In the kitchen Bernie Cooper, dressed for work and scrubbed very clean, pointed towards the table. 'I've put cereals out for you. Do you want toast?'

'No. No. This is fine.' She was not hungry but she slid into the seat and poured milk into the bowl. 'No. This is plenty, thank you. Very kind of you.'

'Isn't it? I know what you're thinkin' you know!'

'What?'

'That I'm some kind of a murderer or a rapist. You think that, don't you?' He was watching her very carefully over the thick rim of his mug. His eyebrows were rough, badger-like.

She met his look. 'Of course not. Don't be daft. But you can't be too careful. There are some creeps about.' She finished eating as quickly as she could, and then asked him how to get to the bus stop. Then she raced upstairs for her bags, keeping an ear open in case he followed up behind her. The doorbell rang and she breathed out. He'd have to answer that himself.

When she came down again Bernie was in the hallway talking to - or rather quarrelling with - a tall young man with the face of a cherub. And golden hair. This boy's bright, wide smile winded Paulie as she came down the stairs. It made light bounce off all the dingy walls.

'What have we here, Uncle Bernie? Don't tell me you've been indulging in a one night stand?'

She saw the smug look on Bernie Cooper's face as he accepted this implicit flattery.

'You couldn't be more wrong,' she said crisply. 'I met your uncle on the train and he offered me shelter. I'm new in this town. Train came in late and he offered me a roof for last night. That's it.' She had to tip her head to meet the man's blue eyes, but she met them. He was even younger than she thought. Eighteen? Nineteen? 'It's not like you think at all.'

'Yeah,' said Bernie gruffly. 'Don't go jumping to conclusions.'

She squeezed past them. Neither of them moved to give her space or to help her with her bags. They closed behind her like the sea, and set away again with their quarrel before she had clicked the door behind her.

She struggled to the bus stop with her bags and had been standing there for ten minutes when the tall, golden haired boy joined her. He held out his hand and flashed his big smile at her. 'That ignorant pig of an uncle of mine didn't introduce us. I'm Charlie Savers, just so you'd know.'

She hesitated then lifted her hand into his. 'Paulie,' she said. 'My name's Paulie.' Her voice sounded weak even in her own ears.

'Paulie? That's a queer old name. Shouldn't it be Pauline?'

'My Dad called me Paulie. That's my name.'

A strand of his long hair lifted in the wind and looked like spun gold in the clear morning sun. She had to pull her glance away from that golden strand of hair. 'You were quarrelling. What was that about?'

He shrugged. 'Bit short of the readies. Mean old bastard's got pots stashed. But he won't part with a single cent.'

She nodded sympathetically. He liked his uncle no more than she did. She managed to wrestle her hand out of his. 'Anyway …' she said, scanning the empty road for a bus.

'Did you say you were looking for digs?' he said suddenly.

'Well. Yes. But first I've got to get to this school.'

'Bernie said you were a schoolteacher. Like no schoolteacher I ever saw, you. Anyway. There's this spare room over at my pad. Promise you, it's legit. The lad who was there. Well. He went away.'

'I have to get this one.' The bus was coming, she held out her hand. 'First day at school. Can't be late.'

'Yes. Yes. Tell you what. Meet you at four fifteen by the market clock. You can't miss it. Centre of town. Here, I'll take your luggage with me. You don't want that stuff in school, do you? I'll meet you at four fifteen and take you to my pad to take a look. At the market clock.' He had violet shadows beneath his eyes and fine blonde stubble which was almost invisible on his fair skin. His pale eyes shone brightly into hers.

The bus stopped and she looked from Charlie Savers to the impatient face of the bus driver. Mesmerised and even now cursing her own stupidity, she left her luggage hostage and climbed on the bus. She peered out of the window and saw the boy standing there, her case in one hand, her book bag in the other.

The head teacher, a smart toby-jug of a woman called Mrs. Townshend, listened sympathetically to her tale of late arrival and offered her the use of an iron in the school kitchens. 'You'd want to be nice and smart for the children dear, wouldn't you?' She put her fingers together and Paulie noted her nails, filbert shaped and polished in pearl pink.

Paulie ironed her blouse and skirt in one of the large, walk-in pantries and presented herself for inspection. Mrs. Toby-jug looked her up and down carefully and nodded. 'Ah, now. That's better, isn't it?' She put on her half-moon glasses and twisted to look at the timetable on the wall behind her. 'I thought you'd like to sit in on Miss Saltbrace this afternoon, Miss Smith. Seven and eight years old, mixed age range. You'll be having this class after the holidays, so it's a good chance to get to know them, don't you think?' She smiled brightly displaying teeth that had been perfectly capped, every one. 'Now you would like that, wouldn't you, Miss Smith?'

No, I wouldn't, you old cow, I'd like to smash all your shiny teeth in. Paulie smiled. 'Yes Mrs. Toby … Miss Townshend. That will be fine.'

The children in the class were curious about her. And they were kind. Miss Saltbrace, who had a tight greybrown perm and a mouth like a steel purse, acted as though Paulie were invisible, so Paulie took her own initiative and went and squatted beside each table to ask the children what they were doing and if she could help.

Her voice barely emerged from the hum of classroom noise, but wherever she was Miss Saltbrace would call across the classroom. 'Table Four, will you stop that noise?' When she went to Table Two, 'Table Two, you are making such a racket!' Then, when she went to Table One. 'Table One, how many times have I to tell you about the noise?'

When the bell rasped through the building for playtime she waited until the children marched out and watched as Miss Saltbrace put the rulers and the pencils in the correct boxes. 'Miss Saltbrace?'

The woman looked at her properly for the first time, high colour staining her face. 'Yes?'

'If you don't want me here I can tell Mrs. Townshend I'd rather not be here, in that case. I can go to another classroom.'

Miss Saltbrace sniffed. 'It's not up to me whether you come here or not.' Her glance went down to her bag, which she was dragging out of the depths of a desk drawer. She checked that her cigarettes were tucked into the side pocket. 'Not my business at all.'

'Oh yes it is. It's you who've treated me like summat the cat brought in. I'm not staying in this room to be treated like that. I'll tell Miss Townshend I'll sit in on another class.'

'I didn't say ...' The woman's rough-edged voice cracked. 'Go and tell the old bonehead, then. Just one more chance for her to persecute me.' Miss Saltbrace bustled towards the door, her sharkskin petticoat screeching against her Crimpeline skirt.

Paulie caught the woman's arm. It felt like lace-covered bread dough. 'Persecuted?'

The woman laughed shrilly. 'Why d'you think I'm going from this place? Early retirement? The chop, Miss Clever! That's what I've had. The chop!'

Paulie trailed Miss Saltbrace down two corridors whose walls were covered with flapping friezes, pockmarked with holes from absent drawing pins. They squeezed past cabinets with rotting nature exhibits and hula-hoops bound together with masking tape.

The staff room was crowded with a dozen or so bodies; the cigarette smoke was being blasted into the air like smoke from a steamer. No one spoke to Paulie, or even looked at her, as she made her way to the messy, cluttered corner where the kettle stood beside a jumble of stained beakers. She made herself coffee, balanced her cup in her hand and went to sit in another corner.

In the rest of the room the teachers sat and stood in clusters and talked of the match last night on the telly and the fate of a young girl on Coronation Street. There were horror stories of the experiences of a nearby school on their HMI inspection, something about some bad report.

The words gyrated round and round her, each word separating from the next and whirling on its own axis.

'Miss Smith. Miss Smith. 'The Toby Jug headmistress eased itself onto the chair beside her. 'How was your morning? Plenty to learn from Miss Saltbrace, I should think.' And Paulie was treated to a malicious smile from Mrs. Townshend's perfect teeth.

Paulie looked across the room to where Miss Saltbrace was emerging from the door marked *Female Toilet*, talcum powder falling from her sleeves and the hem of her skirt onto the threadbare carpet. 'So I have, Mrs. Townshend. So I have.'

By the lunchtime break Paulie felt drained by the acrid taste of despair all around her. Back in the staff room she looked yearningly at the balding carpet. If she could just get her head down on that carpet and sleep for twenty minutes, she would be all right: she would close her eyes and lose all this exhaustion with the smoke and empty chatter.

Still, the staff ignored her. In the end she picked up a battered, three day old newspaper and read about a local bookseller who was in all-out battle with the council over some planning permission. The newspaper was three weeks old.

In the afternoon, she helped the children paint and stick cardboard tubes together. The planned works of art were hedgehogs made by printing hands, and an unnamable machine made of old toilet and kitchen roll centres. Pauline had done exactly the same when she was six. She had seen them done in seven classrooms, in various schools since then. She was suffocating with the darkness of it all. What a mistake. What point was it, if you had kept your

WENDY ROBERTSON

head down in life if you ended up doing this?

At the end of the afternoon Miss Saltbrace spoke to Paulie for the first time. 'Miss Smith? Perhaps you'd like to read the children their story? It's Hansel and Gretel today.' She proffered the battered book with its discoloured cover and left the classroom, handbag clutched under her arm. She clicked the door very deliberately behind her.

Paulie sat on the stool and looked at the large circle of faces around her - some bleary, some bright, all eager. The children were almost licking their lips. She might have been a toffee apple or a particularly succulent hot dog.

She gave her all to the telling of the story. She made use of the book, but all the time she improvised, emphasising the dark dramas of this most perfect fairy tale. She knew she had the children with her. She could feel their fresh-minted interest. Her heart lifted. This was what is was all about, after all. Not Tobyjugs or Steelbraces. It was the best moment of the whole day. As she finished there was a still, gemlike silence: the silence of the spheres.

Then a small girl, pasty face glowing beneath a black fringe, put up her hand. 'Please, Miss?'

Paulie smiled. 'Yes. It's Shalim, isn't it?'

'Yes, Miss.'

'What is it, Shalim?'

'It's not fair, Miss.'

'What's not fair?'

'Well, Miss, people should not eat other people's houses.'

****

Later she had to ask someone, one of the mothers at the gate, the way to the Market Clock. The woman looked up from rebuttoning the misaligned buttons on her daughter's coat. 'Number Two bus, love. Stops across there. Two stops. Can't miss the Market Clock. Town centre.'

As the bus trundled along Paulie pinched her own arms and thighs to see if she were really alive, whether she'd been transformed, in some fairy tale fashion, into bread dough. Or Crimpeline. She was tired, so tired. Too tired, she felt, to face anyone. Even a man whose hair turned to gold in the sunshine. What a mistake it was, to let him have her baggage.

The boy called Charlie was there with a hand-rolled bunch of tulips and lilies that he thrust into her hands   as she stepped off the bus. 'These are for you,' he said. 'Welcome to this bloody godforsaken town.'

The sickly sweet scent of the lilies made her tired senses reel. But still she laughed.   'I thought you were short of the readies?'

'Visited an old pal and he was only too pleased to lend a hand. I told him I had someone to impress.'   He took her arm and steered her across the road, between a red bus and a flat-back truck. 'Not far from here,' he said. 'Not far at all.'

They went along a thoroughfare which was full of Banks and Building Societies, then up narrow streets and alleyways, past the entrance to a derelict garage and a boarded up corner shop.   All the time he talked to her, asking her about her new school and telling her about his own schooldays which he abandoned at fourteen because it was so boring. She told him about Shalim and her particular response to the Hansel and Gretel story. He laughed uproariously at this, but she was certain the irony of the child's answer had escaped him. Perhaps he'd never heard of Hansel and Gretel.* She squashed the instinct to say that maybe they too needed a pathway of crumbs to reach this house of his.   He wouldn't get that either.   He was very young.

'Here!' It was a tall house - four storeys, if you counted the roof window - in a row of tall houses.   There were metal bands and padlocks across all the doors in the row.

'It's a squat!' she said.

'Yeah,' he said, fishing out a key and unfastening the padlock. 'Isn't it great?'

The hall was long and dark and smelled of fish and sweaty trainers.   The boy clicked a switch and a bare, swinging bulb bathed the battered staircase and the peeling walls in a black relief, like the opening shots of an old movie.   She missed the sound of accordions, the hollow clang of bells, and the grind of distant traffic.

He pulled her up the stairs and stood her before a door.   'Now, don't look.'   He put his hands over her eyes. She could hear him opening the door.   He was close behind her, his chest at her back, his knees behind hers.   A benevolent frog march, she thought.   She could smell oranges, patchouli, and lilies and heat.   The room was very hot.

'Now!' He took his hand away.

'Ker- rist!' she whispered, blinking.

The room was lit by forty candles: forty pools of bright light that cast the corners of the tall room into flickering darkness.   In a corner a couch bed hidden by a purple velvet curtain doing service as a throw. More tulips and lilies filled glittering bowls, brass jugs and glass Nescafe jars still with their labels. He had cut the lilies short to get them into the squat jars. A fire was burning in a fine old grate in the centre of the longest wall.

On a low table made of a door mounted on bricks were two bottles of red wine and two tall glasses. Beside that was a tray with pies and a pile of sandwiches. At the far end of the table was a pile of ragged magazines.

'A welcome feast!' He pulled her to the centre of the room. 'Welcome to your new pad.'

'Really. You've gone to so much trouble,' she said uneasily.

'Ah. You think this is the spider's web,' he said. 'The sticky trap. Not really. Look here. A nice room for you yourself.' He walked across and opened a door to reveal a narrow room with a mattress on a platform made of planks, covered with pillows and a duvet with a Batman cover. Beside that was a low shelf made of more planks and bricks, with all her books lined up on it. Against one wall was an intricately carved sideboard with a faded mirror hanging over it. Standing on it, laid out in martial lines, were her own deodorant, her own brushes, her own bag of cotton wool balls.

'You've been in my…' Her glance strayed to a contraption involving hooks and curtain wire. Her own jeans, skirts and blouses hung there. Her own shoes and boots stood below, standing neatly in height order. 'You … thing!' she said. 'You've been into my bags.' Her mind was racing to think of anything in them which might have been embarrassing. 'You shouldn't.'

He was dragging her back into the other room. 'All I was doing was making you comfortable,' he said calmly.

81

'You'll be paying me rent, won't you?'

'Rent? I thought it was a squat.'

'Ah, but there are expenses,' he said. 'Every household has its expenses. Now, sit down there and have your tea. You'll be ready for it, slaving over a hot classroom all day.'

She sat down on the velvet-covered bed, pleased to take the weight off her feet, yet still watchful. He started to open a bottle of wine. She put out a hand. 'Is there tea?'

He looked at her for a second, and then threw up his hands. 'Tea? There'll be tea somewhere.' He went into the other room and she heard him rummaging around. It registered on her that there was no bolt on the door of her little room. Not even a chair to put under the knob. She pulled her coat off, placed it on the couch beside her, and reached up to re-pin her long hair. He glanced at her as he came back in, tea bag in hand. 'Look like a mermaid, you do, in the firelight.' He moved a kettle from the hearth to the fire, and placed a battered teapot onto the mantelpiece. His yellow hair reflected the golden flow of the flames. He turned and flashed his cherubic smile. 'No cooker, of course. Only the light in the hall works. But this'll do us fine.'

Her heart ached at this boy's beauty and ignored her brain, which was telling her not to drop her guard, that there were no reasons why she should trust this golden cherub, any more than she should trust his perspiring, overweight uncle. Or anyone else in this strange town for that matter.

'Can I change my mind,' she smiled. 'Can I try the wine, after all,

14. QUAYSIDE

Paulie: In the end I found an hotel by walking through the town, my bags getting heavier by the minute, back to the railway station. There I stood outside and waited for a taxi to roll up. I put my head through the window. 'Is there a decent hotel you'd recommend? Not too expensive?'

The taxi-driver's eye flickered over me. 'Yes,' she said, 'Jump in.'

She looked at me through the mirror. 'D'you need to be central?'

'Yeah. Near as possible.'

'There's one near the docks. About thirty quid a night? Will that do?'

I made a quick calculation. At that rate John Kebler's advance would not last long. But today had been a long one. One night, just to get my bearings. 'Oh,' I said. 'Yes. Yes. That'll do.'

'It's on the docks. Just a new one tricked up out of an old warehouse. Basic, but OK.'

I wonder what she'd have told me this if she'd know how basic my last 'hotel had been'. There's no flicker in her eyes. She hasn't sussed me either as an ex- prisoner or 'that woman' from the papers. Good thing the papers had to use those six year old photographs.

The journey only takes a few minutes. The blank

front of the hotel belies its neat, pretty interior. The foyer is merely the reception desk plus a circle of sofas. Beyond a screen is a small restaurant, with a self-service buffet at one end, and newspapers on long canes.

The receptionist has long fair hair held back neatly with wide clips. She reminds me of young Lilah. She pushes a registration form across the counter. I sign it swiftly and enter the last address I had with my father, the house where he died. I assume the house is still there. Of course the house didn't burn down. That wasn't the point.

The girl reels off the *modus operandi* of the hotel, which involves as little face to face contact as possible: basically very self-service. She gives me a plastic card. 'That's your room key,' she says. .

I look at it. 'A plastic card?'

'Never used one?' she says. 'It's like this.' She has a mock-up machine on the desk. I'm relieved I'm not the only dumb one. She slides the plastic card up and down in a slot. 'Like this, see? Just do that and it opens.'

Purring up to the fifth floor in the lift I finger the card with some resentment. For six years I've listened to the creak and clank of keys on someone's heavy leather belt, to the grind of the lock, to the turn of the key in someone else's hand. Now here I am on my first night on the out, not even allowed a key of my own.

But the door really truly has a lock: it sounds heavy and solid as it clicks behind me. I play with the heavy latch. Up down. Up down. I lock myself in. I unlock the door. Walk out of the door. I unlock the door, walk through, and lock myself in.

So here I am in my new pad for the night: comfortable double bed; desk with hotel stationery; long mirror. I survey myself. Not too bad, considering. A narrow doorway opens into a smart en-suite bathroom with golden taps and fluffy towels. Television. Radio. Hairdryer. Trouser press. Telephone. This room is small but you have everything. I suppose you might say the same of a prison cell. Only really it really is rather different.

I take my new toiletries out and arrange them, neat as soldiers, along the dressing table. I think of Charlie laying out my stuff. I shake out the new clothes and hang them in the wardrobe. I think of Charlie's makeshift rail. I lay out my volumes of Emily Dickinson and Carol Ann Duffy beside my notebook and on the writing table. I spread out my own slim volumes: one for each of them - Queenie, Christine, Maritza and Lilah. I take my green pen and write in the individual dedications. There, it's done! Now all I have to do is find them so I can hand the books over.

I pick up the phone and dial John Kebler's home number. A woman answers and when I ask for John she asks who I am. In the background a child cries.

'Who are you?' she says.

'Paulie Smith,' I say. 'An acquaintance of John's.'

There is the tiniest of pauses. 'Oh,' she says. 'I see.'

I can hear them talking but I can't hear what they say.

His tone is breezy. 'Paulie? How are you? Where are you?'

'I'm in a little hotel on the docks. Journeyman's Court.'

'The docks? It's all right, Paulie? It's not a ...'

'Knocking shop? Nah. Just a flashed-up commercial place. A step up from a cell, I can tell you.'

'Right. Right. Give me the number.'

'That's why I rang. To give you the number so you can ring me back as soon as you have anything. About Maritza and the rest. I suppose I should get hold of a mobile. When I'm in funds.'

There is a pause at the other end. 'You'll soon run through your money, staying in hotels, Pauline.'

Now I'm mad. 'So where the fuckin' hell am I to stay? In a doss house? Under the bridges like dear old Queenie?' Jail language again. I must watch myself.

'All right. All right. Pipe down.' For the first time ever I hear a thread of irritation in his voice. Then he says, 'Give me that number, Paulie, and I'll ring back within the hour. I have feelers out for those names already and … well, I'll ring you back.'

I give him the number, the phone clicks off and I stare at it for quite a few minutes before I put it down. Now I'm truly alone. In prison you're never alone, yet you're always alone. The only time I didn't feel alone was in those first weeks when I was with Lilah and Queenie and the others from the van. Apart from them I've only really ever known two people in the world. One was my father. The other was Charlie. Both dead now. Dead in fire and smoke. I gag as the smells invade me again: the smell of the room where my father died. I breathe deeply and it goes. The smell of the burnt down house where Charlie died. I breathe deeply and it goes away. It must be a year since those particular hallucinatory smells? images? - what would you call them? - have engulfed me.

Of course I've known some good women in jail. One or two sympathetic officers. One or two understanding teachers. And of course there was the charismatic Stewart Pardoe who inspired me to write. But in jail you learn to keep yourself off - off other people, off depending on them, off leaning on them. You can survive if you keep yourself separate, even though your crowded in with all those others, you have to keep separate. It only works if there is tension, like the filaments on a spider's web. I have to tell you that's the only way to survive in there. On the inside.

I can hear Charlie's voice now, denying that he was setting a spider's web for me.

15 MARRIED BLISS

Maritza: In the suburban *cul de sac* where she'd lived all her married life Maritza Molloy was known as a very quiet woman. She did not join in the coffee mornings; she had nothing to do with the nearby school, even though her two boys had been pupils there between the ages of five and eleven, before going on to the High School. She had nothing to do with the cricket club that butted onto the estate, despite the fact that her husband Desmond had played there most summer weekends since he was fourteen.

Desmond Molloy was known as an altogether jollier person than his wife. He pipped his horn as he swung his flashy car into the narrow road and gave a cheery wave at women wheeling their buggies after their daily walk. On Sundays as he actually walked to the shop for the paper he whistled tunes from the Sixties and occasionally mimed a great bowling action, wind-milling his gangly arms high in the air.

He played in the village cricket team on Saturdays and Sundays, moving to the second team as he slowed down a bit, making way for the young lions, up from the juniors. To call it a Village team was, in fact, a bit of a misnomer as the 'village' had been swallowed up by the nearby industrial town many years ago. Even so strands of village identity persisted. This identity was reinforced by townspeople who'd moved into the village when they reintroduced the village fête, the flower show, and, communal bonfire - all of which had died a perfectly natural death in the 1960s when the mines shut down and the miners moved away.

Maritza had worked in the offices of solicitors Roland Mayor and Partners since she left school, where she'd done quite well in the end, despite being what was fashionable now to call a 'loner'. At Mayor's she was, again, quiet and industrious, advancing in a few years from delivering the post for the partners, to being a very well respected conveyancer, who could be relied on to do a job thoroughly and at speed. She did so well, in fact, that when she had her two boys Roland Mayor made all kinds of accommodations to keep her working there. She worked one, then two, then three days a week.

Then when the boys went on to the High School she returned to full-time work, finishing at four in time for her sons arriving home from the school. She made up for her short days by doing a little extra at Mayor's on Saturdays. The extra time meant she could add wills and probate to her conveyancing.

Desmond was very kind in allowing her to work. He was not disturbed by the arrangement. The house was neat. The meals were on time. His shirts were ironed. They had a cleaner of course. Desmond said he didn't even mind that, as long as Maritza paid her and he didn't have to see and talk to the woman.

As a matter of course, being an accountant, Desmond took care of all the money: her money and his. He conserved it very carefully; even so, no-one could call him mean. He invested in expensive, very tasteful things for the house; mostly antiques that would not lose their value. He collected coins and pushed Maritza into collecting antique jewelry. Those objects, redolent of the lives of women long dead, could not be worn, of course; but you could take them out of the safe and look at them. And they would not lose their value.

Desmond went with Maritza to choose her clothes, often to quite superior designer salons, but always when they were having grand sales and there was true value for money. She was well turned out, a credit to him, in fact. This was despite her not being as sociable as he would have liked. Their two sons were also well turned out. They wanted for nothing. However, in the Molloy household the price of everything was scrutinised and the shrewdest way of purchasing any item was always insisted upon.

She could not accuse Desmond, either, of ignoring her work.

Desmond was obsessively interested in the deals that Maritza handled at Mayor's and often questioned her on the financial details of her work. Her refusal to disclose anything to him owed less to professional discretion, than to the sheer delight at denying him access to something, some part of her life.

She herself was quite interested in the money that swilled around in the accounts that passed across her desk. Unimaginable sums pulsed away there, growing in the dark like mushrooms. Her scrupulous honesty regarding this was outstanding. Mr Mayor remarked on it now and then. When she reminded her boss about some money lying around unused in a client's account, he would pour himself another pot of tea from his teapot and say, 'I can't think what we would do without you, Mrs. Molloy. You are a treasure.'

Maritza had met Desmond Molloy when he joined the accountants who occupied the converted house next door to Mayor's. He was a tall, gangly, curly-haired boy in those days: he was just training for live: making his way, glorious in his whites on Saturdays. From the first he'd liked Maritza's quietness and lady-like demeanour, the way she never called him to order. He could not stand bossy women.

He didn't even react too much when she took him home to the little narrow house with one cold tap and the resting ghost of its previous blind owner. He lived in a council house himself and acknowledged that everyone had to make their way. He certainly intended to.

He got on quite well with Maritza's mother who at that time worked in the same supermarket as his own mother. She started to watch the cricket on television, so she'd have something to talk to Desmond about when he called. She berated Maritza for not watching the cricket. Disloyal, that was, when you thought of it. She told Maritza that Desmond was a nice, steady boy and she'd fallen on her feet with him. Truly, she had. She didn't know her luck. Look at those boys with painted faces and pins through their noses. Would they have been a good choice?

Maritza's brother, home on leave from the navy, thought Desmond was a bit of a twerp but was quite happy to go drinking with him and to fill in as wicket-keeper when the team was one man short.

Maritza went out with Desmond for three years, during two of which they were engaged. The day they bought the engagement ring he set up an account, to which they both contributed. This was to be their savings for the house and for their future lives together.

While they were engaged they kissed and cuddled and petted, but they never went the whole way. When they did make love, on their honeymoon, the experience had an awful sense of anti-climax for Maritza. For her, the kissing, cuddling and petting had been so much more fun than the act of sex itself. Later, when Desmond could legitimately go the whole hog at some speed, he wasn't so keen on the kissing and cuddling and petting. Just the whole hog: that was all he was interested in.

Their sons came along two and three years after the wedding. At least Maritza could kiss and cuddle them, and pet them to her heart's delight. Rory, the oldest endured rather than enjoyed this affection. But Sam, one year younger, lapped it up and even these days, at thirteen, would come up behind her, give her a hug and lighten her heart.

Maritza took some trouble and great pleasure in getting her boys all the toys they ever needed and wanted. She was wandering round a toy shop one day looking for something for Sam's birthday when she came upon a black panda bear with a very seeking face. She took it to the checkout but there was chaos there: something to do with the computer going berserk. Several members of staff were in anxious consultation and a crowd of customers was milling around, angry at the delay. Maritza slipped the bear into her long pocket and walked out, calm on the outside, tense on the inside, breathing freely only when she'd reached the pavement.

When she arrived home she couldn't show the panda to little Sam or his brother. It couldn't be seen in the house. Desmond would want the receipt. Nothing came into the house - not the smallest thing - unless Desmond had the receipt to enter into his all-encompassing financial records.

So the panda went to the very back of the spare bedroom wardrobe, to be joined now and then with all the other small items that seemed to present themselves to her. Lipstick. Bottles of foundation. Brushes. Costume jewellery. Each time she took something a sense of ease flooded into her as she stepped outside the shop. This, she realised, was why she did it. That and the sense of warmth as she touched the pile of things in the wardrobe nestling there beside the panda. The touching gave her comfort and she knew it.

One bright morning at the end of the cricket season, Desmond said, 'We need to talk.' He grinned at himself in the hall mirror, before licking a fragment of cornflake from his left incisor. The team was in the final of some village cup and Desmond had been missing for most of the daylight hours in the previous three weeks,

'Talk?' Maritza was shaking out Rory's blazer which was full of white chalk. He must have been leaning up against some blackboard.

'Yes. A serious talk.' He clicked his briefcase shut. 'Tonight after supper. Rory'll be out at practice.' (Rory was doing very well in the junior team these days.) 'And Sam will be waging world war three with his computer. That boy needs to get out more.'

'What is it?' She said. 'Holidays? I thought we'd already planned…'

'Tonight!' He shrugged himself into the anorak he wore to protect his dark suit in the car. He pecked her cheek. 'Nice flowers these,' he nodded at the tulips and lilies, carefully arranged on the hall table. They caught the light from the window very nicely. The receipt for the flowers was on his spike.

She puzzled about all this declaration. It wasn't like Desmond to be secretive. He was boringly above board, even over the top, about more or less everything. But she had things to do: three fresh probate clients and an exchange of contracts to see to. She wore her best grey suit. So it was that in the rush of the day, the whole matter of Desmond and his few words slipped from her mind.

'I'm leaving you.' Desmond announced at dinner, wiping his mouth with his napkin. 'There's no easy way to say it, Maritza. I'm leaving.'

Her hand, about to put the casserole dish in the dishwasher, arrested in mid-air. 'What? Wha-at?'

'I'm very sorry, Maritza. It's decided.'

She sat down on the floor beside the dishwasher. 'What? What have you decided?'

'Listen to me, Maritza. I'm leaving you. Don't worry. I've taken care of everything. I've bought a house for you and the boys on the other side of ...'

'You've bought a house?' Her skin felt tight. She felt ready to burst like a melon splashed like a hammer.

'I didn't think you'd want to stay here. In any case, there are financial considerations. This house I've bought is more modern than this but it is very ...'

'Why?' She clambered to her feet. 'Why are you doing this?'

Finally, he flushed. 'Well. There is someone...'

'A woman?' A silly question. 'It can't be a woman.

You only show interest in spin bowlers and silly mid-ons. You don't know a thing about sex. Not a thing.'

He was brick-red now. 'No need to be offensive, Maritza.'

She laughed hoarsely. 'No need to be offensive? No need to be offensive? At this minute I find you very offensive Desmond. Who is this woman? Who is this silly mid-on?'

'You don't know her. She's to do with computers. She called at the firm. She's very clever.'

'I don't want to know how clever she is.' She was roaring now. 'I don't want to know.'

'What is it?' Sam was at the door. 'What are you two shouting about? Stop it. You never shout.'

Maritza made herself breathe easier and went to put her arm round Sam. 'You father is leaving us, Sam.' How banal that sounded. Stagey. She looked across at Desmond. 'Now you go. Get out.'

'Be civilised, Maritza. I thought...'

'Civilised?' Her teeth were gritted. 'Get out and leave us alone.'

He was squeezing past her. 'No need to be like this. I've taken care of things. I promise you.'

She and Sam stood with their arms around each other listening to the clatter upstairs as Desmond packed. They were still standing there when he came down with a suit-carrier and a sports bag. He looked at her coolly, his eyes bulging slightly. 'I'll be back for the rest of my things.'

'Make sure I am out.'

'I'll call in at the cricket club and have a word with Rory.'

'Don't be silly. Will you drag him off the crease and tell him you are leaving him? You stupid man. Stupid, stupid man.'

The door clashed behind him and Sam wriggled out of her over-tight grasp. 'Shall I make you a cup of tea?' he said desperately, tears falling down his round cheeks. 'I bet you could do with a cup of tea.'

After that night things moved very fast. The antiques, the jewellery, anything of true value vanished one day when Maritza was at work. A note stuck on the mantelpiece saying they would be sold to meet the expenses of the new house. Their joint account was cleared out. She and the boys were moved to a smaller, meaner house on a smaller, meaner estate on the other side of town.

Desmond had abandoned her. She thought of her father, her beloved Daddy. One day he too had been there; the next he was not. Her mother, she remembered, had packed the whole house into a van.

Through the post she received a neatly written note on thick paper to tell her the exact amount she would be allowed for herself and the boys: the amount was the legal minimum. Her wage from Mayors would be stretched to manage any kind of a life for the three of them.

Mr Mayor, apprised by her of the situation, told her something she didn't know. 'I understand your ... er ... Mr Molloy is moving to Canterbury. Buying a partnership there.'

She flushed. 'I didn't ... know this. Mr Mayor, I knew nothing, nothing of this till three weeks ago.'

The old man shrugged his burly shoulders. 'It seems to happen so much these days. I am at a loss ...'

She stood up. 'I have to get on. There's the Sutton

conveyance to complete. Then I have to shop after work. It's very important that I go to the shops. I need to go to the shops.'

He smiled slightly, relieved that this embarrassing encounter was over. 'Well done, Mrs. Molloy! Work, work, is a great healer.' He leaned to pick up his china teapot and pour out his tea. 'Bravo, my dear! Bravo!

,

16 BUBBLES

Paulie: I rearrange the slim volumes in a different pattern on the desk in my hotel room. Sometimes I put Queenie's copy in the centre; sometimes Mariza's. Then I stop myself. Making patterns of objects is a bad prison habit, bred of the deepest, most profound boredom.

I stand up to make myself a cup of coffee using the immaculate kettle and one of the immaculate china cups. I stretch on the padded chair with my feet up on the bed. Perhaps this is what prison should really be like: an en-suite room like this, complete with television and coffee tray. I'm still chuckling at the impossibility of the thought when the telephone rings.

'Paulie?' It's John Kebler.

'Yes?' I splutter, putting down my cup.

'Paulie?' His voice sharpens. 'Are you all right?'

'Yes!' I am roaring now with laughter, relief tumbling from my lips, relief oozing from the very pores of my body.

'Is there someone else there? Are you drunk?' His voice is anxious now. 'Are you all right?'

I put the phone away from myself and gulp in very, very deep breaths. Then I speak. 'It's all right John. I was just having...' I start to splutter again. 'A fit of hysterics about being here, on the out. You would call it an

anxiety episode,' I roar with laughter again.   He waits.
Then I calm myself down. 'Sorry, John. I lost it for a bit.
I'm all right now.'

'Sure?'

'Sure.'

'Well, listen. I've found a room for you. Cost you
nothing for the time being. Till you get yourself sorted.'

I am totally sober gain. It's true that I'll need
somewhere to stay. My money'll leech away at thirty quid a
night. 'Thanks John. Good of you.'

'I'll pick you up at eleven tomorrow, at the hotel,
and take you there. I'll do some telephoning first thing.
Try to sort something out about those women. Can't
promise anything.'

'Try.' I am hanging onto this thing. I don't think
even he knows how much. 'Try, won't you?'

'I will.' There was a funny note - indulgence? -
kindness? - in his voice. 'Enjoy your first night on the out,
Paulie. Take care.'

I go down to the reception and ask the girl there for
scissors.

'Nail scissors?' she says.

'No. I need them bigger than that. I want to cut my
hair.'

'What?' I might have said I wanted to cut my finger
off. 'There's a hairdresser's in the back street near here.
Marco. He's brilliant.' She swung her own immaculately
barbered bob, demonstrating Marco's brilliance. I think of
Lilah. 'If I rang him … perhaps tomorrow …'

'No. Really.' I am at my most appealing. I smile.
The smile worked all the time in prison. 'I really want to do
it myself. Tonight.'

She shrugged, amusement struggling with disbelief on her face. 'Look. I'll ring the housekeeper.' The housekeeper brings some scissors with red handles. 'Take care, pet,' she says. 'They're very sharp.'

I do handle them carefully. In prison all the scissors are numbered and kept in locked cases. They are counted out and counted back; counted perpetually. Once, in one place where I did time, some scissors went missing and the whole place ground to a halt for a day. Everyone was banged up until they were found, stuffed behind a cabinet. It was never sorted, whether the scissors had got there accidentally or by design.

Now I treat myself to a bath before I cut my hair. Bubbles. Bubbles. The bath is a brilliant sea of bubbles, everyone a bright world in itself. I lower myself into it and stretch. So many firsts. This is my first bath for seven years. I only ever showered on the inside. I didn't trust the baths. You felt vulnerable in a bath. The doors weren't locked.

Bubbles. It's like being reborn. I scrub and scrub with my flannel, getting the gunge of containment, of capture, out of my pores. Shampoo. Conditioner. My hair squeaks in my fingers. I run my hands down my body. I'm as slippery as a seal.

I pull on the fluffy hotel wrap and use one of the white towels to clean the mirror. Now I comb out my hair. Centre parting. Evenly over my head. I daren't cut it too short. I don't fancy a knife and fork special. I draw it all onto the top of my head with an elastic band and cut the bunched hair straight across. I shake it down and I have a fairly decent straight bob. Then I comb the front hair forward and cut the fringe. Then I stretch it dry and flat with the hotel dryer. It is not perfect but as I shake it out and it settles just above my shoulders I know it will do.

I remember the tale young Lilah told, more than once, of how her mother used to iron her long hair flat. On the ironing board, between kitchen paper.

Weird. I have this image in my head - borrowed from Lilah - of that wonderful, loving bond between mother and daughter as Lilah's mother ironed her daughter's long hair between layers of kitchen paper. This is the only real image in my head of devoted motherhood.

17 GOUCHING

Lilah plaited her hair tightly and secured it with an elastic band. She peered into the mirror. Not bad, considering. Eyes in place. Lipstick in place. The bedroom behind her was neat. She still managed to keep it neat, despite everything. This house had been the show house on the estate so had come with curtains, carpets, everything. She had worked hard to keep it that way: the way the developers had displayed it, so they could sell the other thirty-nine houses on the estate to people who wanted nice things around them but were not quite sure how to set about it. As her mother kept saying, they were lucky, she and Jonno, getting this house. Even if they weren't going to get married right away. This house was a very decent start.

There had been a flurry of energy and activity when Lilah announced she was pregnant. Recriminations were quickly followed by kindly practicality. Jonno's parents and her family had clubbed together to put money down on this house. They paid three months' mortgage in advance. It would be a decent place for a baby – their grandchild, after all.

But then she lost the baby and the house was still there; the curtains and the carpets, the customised kitchen. And Jonno. The two of them were bound together now by the little thing that slipped out of her one night and swam away, almost before they realised what was happening, before the pain really hit her: the pain in her body and the pain in her heart.

'You can have another baby, love, in time.' Her mother was all sympathy. 'Just wait a bit and another one will come along.' Being a catholic, she herself had never taken the pill and not by word or deed would she encourage her daughter to do so. She knew things were different now, but as she'd always told her husband, abstinence made the heart grow fonder. Being a good man, after they had their eighth child he took her at her word and turned to beer and snooker to assuage his carnal desires.

Her mother shared with her friends her worry that Lilah had gone right down, since that business with the baby. She had lost weight. Her little face was pinched up. She had no energy. Perhaps it was not surprising. All that rush, then no baby.

In the aftermath of the miscarriage, Lilah had smoked dope for the first time. Jonno urged her. 'It'll take the edge of it all a bit, hon. Make you feel better.' And he'd smoke his stronger stuff and float off in his own little world quite away from her. He would sag on the sofa beside her, eyes closed, muttering now and then. She would come back to her own misery and he would be on his silver cloud and she felt her skin was lined with lead.

At the time of the house, the baby and the miscarriage, Lilah somehow lost touch with her friends Massa, Lynn and Joanna. They moved on to other boys and Alan, Mal and the others brought new girls out with them every Friday night to visit Lilah and Jonno in their new house. Sometimes they brought no girls at all. These days it seemed that girls meant nothing beside the dope and the brown and the feeling of furtive comradeship that floated in the air between Jonno and these lads. They always knew, one way or another, that Jonno would have some gear.

That was when Lilah and Jonno started to have real rows for the first time, about him doing the brown, leaving her stranded on the couch beside him. 'Do it yourself, hon. Nothing like it,' he said easily

'It kills you. It's different from dope. You're a fool to use it Jonno!'

'No! No!' He pulled her to him and pushed the wisps of hair off her brow. 'No. No, hon.' Then he kissed her and it was like the time they first met, when they were dancing till two in the morning at the Sentinel, dancing close but not touching, the thumping beat, joining them together, joining them with all the dancers, everything making sense, everything making peace.

He pulled away from her. 'Try it, Lilah. It'll make you feel better.'

She put her bottom lip out. 'You only say that because you don't like doing it on your own.. You want somebody to gouch with.'

He laughed. 'So what? I'm high. You're high. We'll be high together.' He kissed her again. These days it never went further than kissing. Not since the baby. They had gone on further, just once, but he had rolled away. 'No, Lilah. Not tonight, eh?'

'But…'

'No.'

Now he was watching her keenly, feeling her weakening. 'Try it just once, Lilah. If you don't like it I

104

promise … promise you … I'll never go on at you again.'

She sighed. 'Well…'

'Right! I'll get good stuff, the best. And we'll do it right. Really nice for you.'

They did it right. Closed curtains. Candlelight. Incense. Sitar and bell music on the system. They even had showers, and put on clean clothes. She put a ribbon in her hair. He made the elaborate preparations, urging her to watch, showing her the right way.

The hit that time was almost instantaneous, a wave rippling through her body top to toe, a pulse travelling through her lungs, her heart, her womb, like a coursing shot of velvet lightning. Her knees trembled. He took her hand. 'Sit back, sit back, hon. Let it take.'

The light from the candles swam towards her like bright pearl; the curtains, those tasteful show house curtains, faded to almost nothing. Nothing mattered. Nothing at all. She felt better. So much better.

A hand - it must be Jonno's hand - grasped hers. 'The music, listen to the music, hon!' Then she was the string being plucked by the fingers. Those fingers were making her whole body vibrate. Each note resounded through her and she laughed with the knowledge that the next and the next note were inside her waiting, just waiting to be plucked, to be set free.

Then all the definitions blurred. Seeing. Feeling. Sensing. All these together, running through her, welding together in some hard diamond of sensation. She closed her eyes.

'Now me,' said Jonno. But she didn't hear him.

The weeks after that evening merged into a round of work, house, and waiting for the weekend so it could start again. Jonno was out a lot. His father's taxis ran twenty-four hours so he was out of the house, and in, at odd times. When he was in there were always callers at the house. People always knew they could rely on Jonno for gear.

On three nights each week Lilah would call at her mother's house straight after work. Her mother made her a big plate of egg and chips and told her she should take care of herself. 'You're losing weight, Lilah.'

'Oh, Mum.'

'I know. I know. I shouldn't worry about you. You're your own woman now. But I do worry. Wait till you have your own…' she hesitated.

'My own children,' Lilah smiled. 'Not much chance of that, is there?'

'It doesn't always happen like that, you know. You could try again …'

But the look in her daughter's eyes stopped her. 'Anyway, you should take care of yourself,' she said lamely. 'Eat properly.'

Lilah nodded. The fact was that, apart from these meals from her mother, (hard to keep down), she and Jonno ate little now at home except cornflakes and take-aways. She was always too tired or spaced out to cook.

They did the stuff together now. Sometimes the lads would come and they'd all sit round and do it together. Lying back and muttering, staggering about the place, coming to now and then to crash another CD into the machine. Sometimes the television would be on and they would change stations to ensure a continuation of the soaps, which were their absolute favourite. Familiar faces doing familiar things.

In time she had to take more and more of the stuff to get any kind of hit. But it stayed worth it. She knew she would be so outside it all, so alone, if she stayed off it in Jonno's company. She only did it for company. She could come off it any time. She knew that.

Work was getting a bit of a burden, too. Getting there for seven-thirty occasionally seemed impossible. She had two warnings for being late. And concentrating on the intricate wiring became increasingly difficult. Especially in the afternoons.

One night she came back from her mother's early, to find Jonno and Alan Newton on the sofa, beside them the dull shine of foil, the gleam of a needle. She caught Alan by the scruff of his coat. 'Out! Out! Fucking crack-head. Out! Out!'

Alan was heavy, hard to shift. She let him drop back to the couch and raced upstairs. She threw herself on the bed and lay there and looked at the white ceiling. She got up, drew the curtains and put on the lamp. Then she lay back again on the bed and watched the effect of the light on the ceiling. That was it. She and Jonno were finished. Now he was digging. If he didn't stop that they were finished.

She didn't speak to Jonno the next day, or the next. She slept in for two days running and was late for work. The day after that, a Friday, her foreman called her to his narrow office at the edge of the shop floor. He pushed an envelope over the scarred desk. 'That's your notice, Lilah. Four week's pay.'

'My notice, but…?'

He waved a hand. 'You've had warnings Lilah. More times late than early. And your work's right off.

Line leader says you've stopped the line, four times.'

'But, that's not fair, I…'

'Like I say, you've had your warnings.'

She was still crying when she reached her mother's house.   Her mother put her arms around her.   Her daughter felt fragile, like some starving bird.   'What is it, pet? What is it? Is it that Jonno? I tell you I…'

'I've got the sack from work,' mumbled Lilah. 'They've sacked me.'

'Sacked you? What for?'

'Lateness. Bad work.'

'But that's not fair.   You've not been well since, since that happened about the baby.   Look at you.   Not a picking on you. Must have lost two stones.' She pushed her tenderly onto the kitchen chair.   'You sit there, pet. I'll make you a nice cup of tea.'

That night Jonno did not give Lilah time to tell him her bad news. 'Bad news, hon!' he said.

'Bad news?' she said.

'Yeah.   Got copped today.   Banned for a year.'

'You in court? Today?'

'It happened a while ago. Last month.   Didn't want to worry you. Caught and breathalysed. Third time. One year ban.   My Dad's furious.   Can't drive his cabs any more.'

'The office. Can't you work in there?'

Jonno shook his head. 'My dad's not interested. Kicked me out, lock, stock and barrel.   Someone told him about the other stuff, not just the booze. Never darken my doorstep, all that stuff. He's a wanker.'

Then she told him her own news.   'So how'll we pay the bills, the mortgage?'   she said soberly.   'It's all over.

Jonno.'

Jonno looked at her, looked at her afresh for the first time for a year. 'You've lost weight,' he said.

'My Mum said that too.'

'I'll make you a cup of tea,' he said. 'You just sit there.'

The next day when she woke up she was shivering all over. Her head was aching, her legs were aching, the very organs of her body were aching. She went to the toilet to be sick and found Jonno there with his head in the toilet bowl. He got up and washed his hands and face.

'A bug,' she said wearily, 'We must have caught a bug.' Then she retched and he made room for her.

Later, they were sitting quietly round the kitchen table in a very fragile state when the back door rattled and Alan bowled in. 'Whatsa matter with you two?' he said. 'You look like death warmed up.'

Lilah put her hand to her mouth. 'We've caught this heavy bug. Aching all over. Sick. Never felt like this before.'

He looked from one to the other and grinned. Then he pulled a small packet from his pocket and slapped it on the table. 'Well, here, friends, I have your medicine. Top quality gear. A smoke of this will cure anything. Migraine. The pox. May ye suffer no more! Medicine, my children.'

Lilah was so bone-weary she hardly noticed the deft way Alan went about his operations. She snorted her line distractedly, without the usual focused excitement.

She only knew that this time the hit did not involve kaleidoscopes of colour or pulsating curtains. She did know that within minutes of the hit all her aches and pains and nausea were gone. She felt better than she'd felt in weeks. Her mind was clear. She could think clearly.

The same was happening to Jonno. 'D'you say you got four weeks' pay?' he said, lying back in the chair.

Lilah nodded.

'Well all we have to do is buy gear with it, keep our own stash, pass it down the line, and we'll have our first stake. That'll pay the mortgage. And the bills.' It seemed easy, logical, the way he said it. And anyway it was so nice, so good, to be without without the pain.

That was when, for Lilah, the hits lost their ritualistic preparation, their anticipation of paradise, and became the administration of medicine for chronic and increasing pain.

Lilah was not sure whether the knocking was inside her head or outside it. She rubbed her forehead hard and pulled herself to the side of the bed. She peered through the curtains, blinked in the bright sunshine and saw the round figure of her mother at the front door. 'It's my mother.'

'You see to her,' from the lump under the blankets. 'Go and get rid of her.'

The banging continued.

Lilah stumbled to the bathroom and swabbed her face. She pulled her hair back on an elastic band and pulled a cotton wrap over her long T-shirt.

The banging continued.

'Coming, coming!'

She opened the door. Her mother stood there in leggings and a bright ski jacket, a roomy leather bag over her shoulder. 'I was just on my way to the shops,' she said brightly. 'I just thought I'd call in.'

Lilah opened the door wider. She yawned. 'I'll put the kettle on,' she said. She led her mother to the kitchen, which was slightly tidier than the sitting room. That was strewn with cans and works and God knew what. Her mother took the kettle from her hand. 'Here. Let me make it.' Lilah sat and let her mother make the tea. Allowed her to pour it.

'You don't look too grand,' said her mother at last. 'In fact, you look awful.'

'We've had flu. Both of us,' said Lilah, looking into her cup. 'I couldn't call down…'

'I thought something must be up, you not calling,' said her mother.

Lilah drank her tea and looked at the way the sun caught the spoons which were standing upright in a jar on the windowsill.

Her mother took her hand. 'I was talking to Doctor Wainwright, love.'

'What about? Are you poorly?'

'About you. And your … flu.'

'What about it?'

'Well, your sisters and your brothers know about it. This flu. They told me. Is the mother the last to know? Anyway, they know.'

'Do they?' Hardly surprising.

'Anyway, Doctor Wainwright says he can help.'

Lilah shook her head. 'No need. I'm all right.'

Her mother clasped her hand more tightly. 'Your brother says that he – your Jonno -well, he sells it. That you sell it. That stuff.' For the first time her voice shook. 'Lilah … I …'

Lilah wrenched herself from her mother's grasp.

'We're all right, Mum. We're just a bit down because we've lost our jobs. And we've got the flu.' She stood up. 'Thanks for calling, Mum.' She stood by the door. 'But maybe you could ring next time? We never know when we'll be in.'

Through a crack in the sitting room curtain Lilah watched her mother click down the overgrown path in the limpid sunshine. The yellow and green of her jacket was unbearably bright.

'Was that your mother?'

She turned around wearily. 'Yes, it was.' She looked round the cluttered room. Jonno was standing in the doorway in just his pants. She could see his ribs. 'Jonno, this place is a mess. We need to clean it up,' she said dully.

Jonno looked at her and nodded. 'Yeah, yeah, hon. I tell you what, we'll have a big clean up. I'll get the Hoover and you can start on the kitchen. Open those curtains, hon. Let a bit of light in.

18 BRIEF ENCOUNTER

Paulie: The hotel mirror is being very kind to me. With my new long bob, my new clothes, make-up, I am very different - glossier, more essentially measured. I look at the scissors. It's so tempting to keep them, to tuck them into my bag. Inside they'd have been worth quite a packet of one thing or another. Christine would have given her eye teeth for nice sharp clean scissors.

But now the double-take of the receptionist as I return the scissors rewards me for leaving that thought behind. 'Not bad!' she says approvingly leaning across to flick the ends of my hair. I steel myself not to recoil. 'No one'd even think you'd done it yourself.' The hotel only does breakfasts, so she tells me about two restaurants on the quayside and a pub that does reasonable bar food.

It's quite early in the evening, so the pub is just about deserted. I go to the bar, get some coke and read the menu carefully. Choice! Another great freedom. I choose Caesar salad to celebrate the availability of fresh vegetables and take a seat by the window. I become mesmerised by the shimmering movement, the sheer variety and colour of people as they pass; the blinding light reflected in the wide river as it churns its way to the sea. And from where I sit, I can see three bridges channelling people in cars, on trains in their free, free movement to and fro - movement which they have chosen themselves.

'Can I sit here?'

I look up with a start. A tall girl with a long face and a very smart over-fitted leather jacket is smiling down at me. (I ordered a biography of Virginia Woolf once, from the prison library. The biographer seemed totally in love with her subject. This woman has a Virginia Woolf face: elongated with amazing brows.)

'Is this seat taken?'

I glance round. The bar has filled up while I've been daydreaming. 'Sure. That's all right.' My voice is awkward. My lips seem to be made of very thick rubber.

She settles herself down, and looks directly at me, then at my plate. 'What did you have? Was it OK?'

I look down at my plate, prison-clean. 'Er ... Caesar salad. It was very good. I didn't think pubs did that kind of food.'

She raises her finely arched brows. Her face has the large eyed beauty, the elegance, of a well-bred dog. A greyhound, maybe. 'It's not uncommon. Have you been away?'

I nod. 'Yeah. I've been away.'

She gives her order then flips a glance across at me. 'Can I get you a drink? You can keep me company while I try to render up to Caesar that Caesar salad.'

I can't say no. I can't get the words together to refuse this woman. I nod dumbly.

She picks at the salad and leads the conversation. She makes me lie about having been in hospital...

'... I thought you looked pale.' Her tone is warm, reassuring. The toe of her boot touches mine.

Oh-oh. Where have I been? It's a pitch. In prison,

it's no problem telling one of these girls they're off on the wrong foot. But how do you do it here? In the middle of a crowded bar with a very personable girl who can say ten words to every one of yours? I pull my foot away from hers. 'So what is it you do?' I say desperately. 'Do you work in the town?'

She nods and sips her red wine. 'I am a cataloguer at the Central Library.'

'That must be interesting,' I say lamely.

She smiles her elegant smile. 'Kind of you to say.'

A girl in jeans and a red T-shirt comes and takes our dishes away. The woman leans across and puts her large capable hand on my forearm. 'Can I get you another drink, or would you like to go somewhere else? There are some great places in this town.'

I look at the hand and my mind flips back to the time when I kneed Bernie, Charlie's uncle, in the crotch to stop his predatory advance. I take a breath.

The word is mightier than the sword. I stare at her hand. 'I should come clean, really,' I said. 'It's not hospital I've been to. I'm just out of prison. And I do know how to put off unwanted advances in there. But to be honest, I'm not sure of the protocol of doing that on the out.'

She looks at me hard, to see whether I am joking, then takes her hand away. She chuckles. 'Sorry, sweetheart. My mistake. I was mistaking confusion for signals.' She sat back. 'But still, would you like a drink? You can hardly run off now in maidenly disarray. To show no hard feelings?'

I smile and relax. 'Let me get one for you,' I say, 'To show no hard feelings.' I feel her eye on me as I walk to the bar.

So the two of us have a jolly night. She gets steadily more maudlin on red wine; I stolidly keep her company drinking Coca Cola. Like the reporters she's too interested in life inside and I put her off with generalities. I ask her about films and music, what the It-girl is watching in this millennium year. What is she reading?'

'Books? Darling! The last book I read was *White Fang* in High School. The book was a bore but the woman who taught us was a darling.'

She walks me back to the hotel and asks to come in for just a night-cap after such a good time. She is too close. Gently I push her away from me. 'What? I wouldn't trust you over my threshold. I wouldn't be safe.'

We both laugh at this and part the best of friends. She gives me her card and tells me to ring her, any time. It's only when I've stripped off and am having yet another bubble bath that I realise that I don't know her name, nor she mine. I rise dripping from the bath and scrabble in my pocket for the card. Sasschia Colbourne. Three' SS's'! Such excess. I wonder if she invented it. It seems very false. I tear the card up to small pieces and throw them one by one, into the waste bin. Then I turn on the hot tap to warm the water and step back into the bubbles. Again.

19 COMING TOGETHER

Five Women: The van smelled of ammonia mingled with that kind of room freshener which fills the air with the dying moan of flowers.

Maritza stared dully at the grille before her and settled down on her seat. The face and form of her son Sam printed itself onto the grill, and then faded as fast as it came. Rory refused to come to her properly. There he was - tall, like his father with his thatch of mud-coloured hair. But she could not make out his face. She could not see him as a person.

She shook her head, dislodging thoughts of both her sons. The two them were safe enough now with her mother. She'd seemed momentarily entertained at the thought of stepping into the breach and taking the boys into her house, having them under her charge. Maritza thought that in the place where she was going she'd have to learn not to think of them in her mother's house: She needed to make her mind blank.

The pain of missing her two sons added a sharp edge to the dull pain, the disabled, inner fury that had suffused her body for days and then had intensified when, at the magistrate's request, the officer had 'taken her down'.

Now, very deliberately she focused on the here and now in this in this sealed white van, which had stopped creaking. Everyone must be on board. This was clearly a world of hard edges. Grilles. Cords. Steel with an edge rubbed off here and there to rust in a friendly fashion. The Group Four officer was a slight woman. You'd never know she was a Judo Black Belt, though that was the first thing she'd told Maritza in the corridor by the police cells. Perhaps she told everyone, to pre-empt any hassle. She bounced onto the step and called the names, referring to a list on a fluttery piece of paper.

'Cazalet, Christine?'

'Yes!'

'Smith, Paulie? Paulie? Smith?'

'Yes!'

'Pickering, Queenie?'

There was a pause.

'Pickering?'

The officer jumped onto the van and put her head over the first door, then recoiled a little at the smell. 'Pickering?' she said, to the old woman who was sitting there, strapped in.

'Where's my other bag?' said Queenie.

'You're only allowed one bag.'

'Ha! You know he came and took it.   Took it and flew away with it, cackling, I saw him!'

'Who?'

'The Devil.'

Judo Black Belt smiled faintly.   'You're a barmy old bugger aren't you? Shouldn't be going to this nick. Not the place for you. Nut house, more like.'

'He took my bag, the old Devil.   Had a wingspan of at least forty feet.'

'Pickering.'   Black Belt ticked the name. 'Molloy, Maritza?'

'Yes!' The sounding of her name followed by the bald surname-Desmond's name- made the hair on Maritza's neck prickle.

'Rutherford, Lilah?'

'Yes!' said Lilah, clutching the metal arms of the seat. The sweat was already beading up on her forehead. She was in pain. Never had she been in so much pain. She'd had nothing - no stuff, not even methadone, not even codeine, since they arrested her two days ago. Not in the police cell, not at the court. In court she'd only felt like crying out once, when she saw Jonno wearing his big coat in the gallery, sprawling there with Alan Smith beside him. Jonno caught her eye and smiled and nodded. Then, after carefully glancing round the court, he'd shaken his head from side to side. Say nothing!

Lilah had pleaded innocence, ignorance, to the stolid, low key questions of the prosecuting solicitor. She was not helped at all by her own solicitor who appeared to be proceeding on automatic pilot. So Maritza was remanded in custody until her trial.

'Oh no, Lilah!' Someone at the back of the court had groaned then. Lilah's head went up, towards the back row of the gallery. There was her mother, bright coated and white-faced. Lilah wondered why her mother had even bothered to come. It was months since she'd seen her. How many days had Lilah hidden in the house and not responded to her mother's knock? She shouldn't have come to court. Stupid woman.

The van jerked and another wave of pain hit Lilah, making her stop thinking of anything else, any other thing, and any other time. Her armpits ached. The very inside of her eyelids winced with pain as the door clanged shut.

Each of the women was in her own steel cubicle, behind her own steel doors. The driver released the handbrake and the heavy van, hesitating on its brakes at first, embarked on its journey to the prison. Christine settled in her cubicle and waited till they were on the smooth road.   'Here we go,' she said cheerfully, loudly. 'Back to the land that time forgot.'

Then the only sound they could hear was the roar of the engine and the muffled twang of the van radio. Then Maritza said, 'Have you been there before, then?' Her voice sounded thin, wavering ears like wisps of smoke in the stifling air of the van.

'A couple of times,' Christine's young voice was tough with distilled nonchalance. 'How about you? You done time?'

Maritza clung onto the bar as the van swung round a corner.   The iron seat bar rammed itself into her back. There'd be a bruise there for sure. 'No. Never. Never anything like this.'

'Anyone else?' called Christine. 'Been in before?'

For minutes the only thing any of them could feel was the numbing vibration of the metal. Maritza thrust away an image of Sam that had started to form on the grill again. 'So what about you? What got you here?' she said.

Christine roared with laughter. 'Let me tell you sommat, love. Anyone can tell you've never been inside. Here's a tip for you.   Never, never ask someone why they're there.   And if you're asked, don't tell them. Make sommat up.'

'Why?'

'You just don't. Any case, they'll find out in time. But don't tell them - officer, inmate, cook or clerk. Don't say.'

Christine sat back, closed her eyes and allowed herself to be overtaken by the jerking rhythm of the van. You soon learn that you shouldn't tell. What happened to Tigger had taught her that.

Someone had told on Tigger. She'd met her old friend Tigger again on her second time inside. Tigger was in for attacking a policeman again outside the pub with too much vodka inside her. Bloke tried to touch her up so she'd treated the joker to a black eye.

Christine had spotted Tigger across the dining room. Tigger yelled 'Ye-es! Fuckin' Chris-tine, that's who it is!' And she had belted across the echoing space to say Hello! Hello! The two of them danced around and around, arms linked, under the eagle eye of the staff. An officer started to stroll across and they quietened down and went to sit at one of the tables side by side. Tigger, eighteen now, looked no different: slight, monkey-faced with that wide, cute grin. They'd chattered then, exchanged tales about coming up against the heavy-handed cops, running, doling about, the booze and drugs.

'Still hurtin' yourself?' said Tigger, looking at Christine's bandages.

Christine pulled down the sleeves of her cardigan. 'It comes and goes,' she said.

Then they were called back to their cells and locked in till six. Christine lay on her bunk and ignored her current pad-mate, thinking of the good times she and Tigger had enjoyed in that big house: climbing up trees like lads. Smoking dope. Playing snooker. Tigger, when she thought of it now, had been the only one, the only one who ever knew her.

She saw Tigger again at Association the following night. And the next. The days stretched out to the length of a week. Every day, with the other silent girl in the cell, Christine cleaned the narrow space. Blankets folded military fashion. Walls. Sink. Lavatory bowl shining. One day the officer who inspected the cell picked imaginary fluff off the top of the curtain rail and asked them if they'd bothered to clean that morning.

Her wristwatch was still there in Reception, so she didn't know the time. Her pad-mate hid hers under her jumper. The day consisted of long stretches of sleep, breakfast and dinner on plastic plates, a visit from the teacher who took her through the usual questions and asked if she would like to sign up for some cell studies. And more sleep.

Then at last, tea and Association. One day she looked eagerly round the long room for Tigger. She wasn't there. 'Where's Tigger?' she asked one of the women, a heavy woman who seemed to roll rather than walk about the place.

The woman winked, 'Yeh know that little pervert, then? Nonce, that one.'

'Pervert? Tigger?' Her fists curled. 'What yer bloody saying? She ain't no pervert.'

'Not what I hear.'

'Well ye're goin' deaf then.'

'You watch it, or you'll get done yerself,' the woman growled.

'Done? They hurt her?'

The woman shrugged her massive shoulders. 'Wouldn't do it meself but … what can the lass expect?'

Christine put her hand out to grasp the woman's arm

122

and thought better of it. 'So what is it she's supposed to have done?'

'Only took some kids off, that she was babysitting.'

'Took them off?'

'Aye. Drowned one of them in a river. One of the lasses had a visit from her sister and she said it was all in the paper.' The woman cupped her hand to take the ash dropping from her roll-up. 'Deserves anything she gets, that one. Pervert.'

Christine opened her mouth the protest, and then closed it. Then she said, 'Is she shut in on the Wing?'

'Nah. She's down in Seg. Behind the door. They're keepin' her safe. But what they want to keep her safe from, I don't fuckin' know. Deserves whatever comes to her. Nonce.'

That night the women in that prison set up a shouting howl, yelling threats towards Tigger through the bars into the night. Lying on her bunk, Christine's flesh chilled to freezing. The group of women in there - tall, short, fat, thin, ugly, beautiful - seemed the same as any group of youngish women on any Wing, in any town, on any street. But at night when the shouting started, the voices hoarsened in the night air and joined together into a single wild roar of threat. A single beast.

Christine had covered her head with the blanket, ignoring her pad-mate, who was up with the others, shouting about just what she would do to anyone who hurt children and deserved everything she got. There was clear consensus in the crowd that anyone who hurt children should be put down for her own good.

She lay awake all night and the next day, when they

were cleaning the cell her pad-mate told her to buck up. At this rate they'd still be cleaning when the fucking officer came and anyway why was she working only with one hand? She reached over and took Christine's left hand and pushed back the sleeve of her sweatshirt. She dropped the dripping hand. 'Fuckin' hell. What'yer at, lass?' She leaned over and pressed the panic button. It took five minutes for an officer to get there.

'What is it?' The officer, Mrs. Courtney, was a solid, capable woman who liked the job, but had learned early on to keep her face in a still mask.

'That lass!' The girl indicated Christine crouched up on the top bunk. 'Get her out of here. Look at her hand. She's fuckin' burnt herself.'

Mrs. Courtney pulled at the hand and surveyed the mass of blisters. 'Well now, you'll get no tobacco after this, lady. Waste of a good fag.'

Christine was taken to the hospital wing to get the hand properly dressed. The doctor talked to her. The nurse talked to her, but she would not talk back. She would tell them nothing. She was being escorted back to her room when she glimpsed Tigger, lounging pale-faced on a bed talking to the woman Christine recognised as the teacher. Tigger had a livid bruise on her cheek.

She stopped and leaned round the door. 'You all right Tigger?' she said.

Tigger had smiled wanly, 'Survivin',' she said. 'Just about.'

The nurse behind Christine had dug her in the ribs. 'Come on, Cazalet. We haven't got all day. Don't waste time talking to that...'

Afterwards it turned out that Tigger had gone

through all that for nothing. It was in the papers six months later. Tigger got off the charge because it turns out she'd been set up by the brother of the kids. He'd done it but because of her background she was the likely one. So she was the one who got arrested, the one who got beaten up, the one that spent her six months remand in segregation where even the officers who protected her despised her..

When she got out that time Christine had tried to find Tigger but she wasn't sure how you went about it and gave up after a week.

The white van swerved round a corner and Lilah groaned.

'You all right, kid?' said Christine.

Another muffled moan.

Christine remembered the fleshless face, the big eyes of the girl who'd dragged herself on the van. 'Junkie,' she said. 'I was forgettin'. Well, darlin', you'll get worse in there, love, before you get fuckin' better.'

Lilah groaned again.

'You never been in, have yer?'

'No,' groaned Lilah.

'Well then, don't expect no sympathy from them doctors. You'd get more sympathy out of a fuckin' lollypop man's stick, I'm tellin' yer.'

Lilah managed to speak. 'Some help, that.'

'Don't mention it. Forewarned is forearmed. That's what I say, darlin'.'

Paulie listened to the shouted conversation in frozen silence. Ever since that final moment in court, she'd been waiting for the feeling of despair, of panic, to come down on her, the final reality of what had happened. Oh, she knew in words what had happened! *Remand in custody....* *Preparation of the case* ... Her solicitor had said it would take some time. It always did, in these serious cases. 'Just settle down and have a rest,' he said. 'I know that sounds strange but it's not impossible. Just keep your head down. I'll come and see you, tell you what's happening. There'll be depositions. Important that you see a psychiatrist. Perhaps more than one.'

Paulie had looked at him. He was a small, full-faced man, with a beard, but no moustache. You had the feeling that if you turned him upside down he'd look just the same. But he'd been kind enough with her. Open. Respecting her intelligence. Pulling no punches. But still, he'd been too optimistic. 'The whole thing is circumstantial. It's too easy for them to pinpoint you. Too easy by far. We'll challenge it, be sure of that.'

She almost didn't care. At least it had all stopped. She'd stepped off the roundabout. Or been pushed off it. She realised it now how easy it had been to step on that roundabout into Charlie's arms. With him life had been a bright flawed dream, whirling around there, pulsing with love and laughter. So easy.

Charlie, in those early days, had been so beautiful, so anxious to please, so difficult to leave in the mornings, his long limbs twining round the rumpled sheets on her bed. 'Come back, come back, you gorgeous thing. It's too cold in here without you.'

She began to worry in case they would smell it on her at school. Not just the sex, but the honey-scent of heightened feeling, the fruity sense of fulfillment. But no.

As the weeks and months went on the other teachers actually began to let her in on their conversation, despite being disappointed that she never watched the soaps or even the odd episode of Midsomer Murders. 'You should watch it, dear. Very true to life.'

They did tend to wonder how she spent her time. How boring must her evenings be! She could hardly tell them she'd been smoking weed and listening to thin music on Charlie's iPod, that she had strolled by the canal in the dark, walking along the safety wall and jumping off into the arms of a young man who looked like a Botticelli angel in torn jeans and big boots.

She couldn't tell them that she couldn't watch telly because in this haven, this paradise of the senses, there was no electricity: only the guttering light and warmth of candles and the red flare of the fire. She and Charlie fed the fire with coal and logs that he brought in his sports bag after foraging in other people's back yards. And the floorboards from the top floor of the squat came in handy when they were desperate.

It was not that they were short of money. There was money around. They had money. Within a month or so she had her wages and he never seemed short of cash. 'Where do you get it?' she said once.

'For me to know and you to find out,' he told her, and kissed her to close her mouth. He showed her fine drawings he'd made of elaborate monsters and fiends with dripping fangs; he showed her poems that he had written. He waited with uncharacteristic uncertainty for her comment. She saw the look in his eye and told him they were all wonderful, although she knew they were rubbish, loaded with banal sentiment and bottom heavy with pathos.

He told her he had never met anyone like her: that they'd always be together. Always.

He had a couple of friends who came round every few weeks and they would smoke joints, do lines of cocaine and spend evenings in mumbling, complacent camaraderie. When this happened she shut herself in her room, turned up her battery radio and read her book. Despite Charlie's angelic charm and his vows of undying love she felt no responsibility for him whatsoever. It was his life. Let him do with it what he wished.

Then one day before setting out for school in the morning she'd had to climb over the boys' bodies to get out and grabbed a sandwich and a coke at the corner shop for her breakfast. Paulie had quite enjoyed the feeling of her two lives so completely enclosed from each other: her life at school where, because of her hard work, she was being considered for a sort of special responsibility; and life with Charlie which was whoozy and undefined with no responsibility at all.

Then one day Charlie was arrested and charged with snatching money from some man as he came away from a bank machine. The man had his wits about him and called the police on his mobile phone. The police caught Charlie running like a hare five streets away. But he had no money on him and the robbed man didn't spot him in the line-up. He was finally released because of this problem over identification.

While he was in custody Bernie Cooper, Charlie's uncle had come to see Paulie. 'The police got him. There's gunna be a line-up. They'll not really get him, like. He's a sly one, young Charlie. Always was.' He glanced round the squat, which looked squalid in the daylight, the candles cold and black, spilling over in their jars. 'You'll want to get out of this pig-hole. Come to my place, I'll tek care of yer.'

'No. No,' she said. 'I'll stay here. It's all right.'

Then, at a speed surprising for his bulk, he was at her side of the room and had her against the wall. 'What you want, lady, is not so much taking care of, as a good seeing to.'

He was pulling at her clothes and holding her at the same time. She relaxed until she was very slack and his lips were on hers, his snakey tongue forcing its way into her mouth. Then she focused all her will on her booted foot and the strength of her knee and her thigh. Then she brought up her knee right into up into his crotch. He fell off her howling. 'You little bitch,' he yelped.

She leaned over to pick up a paring knife that had been on the table for a week. Charlie had used it to cut up a pineapple that he'd scored off a market stall. It was a tough old pineapple and had needed a very sharp knife. She brought the knife up in front of her and said to Bernie, 'Now get out of here, or I'll stick you as easily as I'd stick any other pig.'

He stumbled off, clutching himself. When Charlie came back a day later chortling with delight over the aborted identity parade, she didn't mention his uncle coming to the squat. That was her business, not his. She had dealt with it.

They celebrated his release with a twenty quid meal for two from the Chinese Take-away, washed down with three bottles of wine in the candle-light. He told her macabre tales of the police cells and how the boys in blue had been determined to pin the robbery on him.

'But you did it, didn't you?'

'Ah, that's by the way, my darlin'. Point is, can they prove it? Anyway, I didn't do it, because I didn't score the money. Some old feller down the allotments'll be counting the notes now, thinking there's fairies at the bottom of his garden. I threw it over his fence.'

She kicked his ankle with her bare foot. 'You didn't tell me that's how you got your money, you villain.'

He shrugged. 'You never asked me.' He peered closer at her in the light of the guttering candles. 'Fact is, you don't seem curious about nothing.'

'Don't I?' She moved, curling up so her knees were nearly under her chin. 'Why should I be?'

''Cause it's like … it's human to be … like… curious. To be critical, like.'

'Oh, me! Didn't you know I'm not human? I come from outer space,' she yawned, 'though why I landed on this boring planet I can't tell you.'

He looked at her for a minute then gulped wine from the neck of the bottle. 'Well, anyway. There's no scoring for me for a while. You should'a seen their look when they had to let me go! Still, there's the money from your job, so no problem.'

A week later a child came to her with a note from the head teacher, telling her to please come to see her at the end of the lesson.

Later, as the kids roared their playtime chants outside she sat in a narrow chair, looking at the head teacher across her neat desk.

'Miss Smith, this is quite difficult for me to say...'

'Yes? What's difficult? Has there been an accident or something?' Paulie frowned.

Miss Townshend shook her head. 'Miss Smith. Do you enjoy your work?'

'It's all right. The children ... I like the children.'

'Your children's work is quite good.' The other woman's tone was grudging. 'Progress being made has been remarkable...'

'Well. What is it Miss Townshend?' She allowed her tone to be sharp.

'You seem not to ... well, talk to your colleagues very much. You're seen as very distant.'

Paulie shrugged. 'I don't have that much to say to them. To be quite honest we haven't got much in common. They don't talk to me much. Seems like my problem is I don't have a telly and don't do pub quizzes.'

Miss Townshend looked down at a note in front of her. 'You live at number seventeen Barney Row, Miss Smith?'

'That's right.'

The head teacher drew a deep breath. 'I had the occasion to drive past it. Yesterday. After school.' (It had taken her some time, but she'd found it.)

'Yes?' What was the woman getting at?

'It was boarded up. There were padlocks on the door. It looked...'

'They call it a squat, Miss Townshend,' said Paulie patiently. 'Derelict building used for accommodation. Helps with the housing shortage. No harm done. Nobody really worries. Then they come to demolish it and build a superstore or a garage and people move out.'

'It's really not suitable...'

Paulie stared at her. 'There was nothing in my contract that stipulated where I live, Miss Townshend.'

Miss Townshend pushed a folded piece of paper across the table towards her. 'This came in my post on Monday. Read it.'

The letters were painstaking, as though a child had written them. But from what the words said, - about the Teacher Miss Smith living in a Squat which was really a Brothel and a haunt for Drug Dealers.... - It was quite clearly the work of an adult. It went on... *A place that the police raided and where people were. Arrested for mugging decent hard working folks. Anyone who lived in such a place had no right to have Responsibility for Children.'*

'Your correspondent is illiterate as well as ignorant,' Paulie said, pushing the paper back. She knew perfectly well who the correspondent was. 'And he has no right to say such things.'

The woman looked at her narrowly. 'He? Are these things true?'

'Do you believe them?'

'As I told you I went to see the house. It certainly looks like a ... squat, did you call it?'

'So what did you want me to do about it?'

'Miss Smith, your manner... I don't care for your manner.'

'It was a genuine question, MIss Townshend. What do you want me to do about it?'

'I am at a loss that you don't know what you should do. The parents of the children in this school, the governors, they would all be shocked...'

'Will you tell them?'

'If I kept it from them I would be as guilty as you, of living a lie.'

'Come on! I didn't lie to you.'

132

'You did, by implication. No normal teacher would…'

Paulie was very weary. 'Normal teacher?' She stood up. 'Oh, go fuck your school and your mealy-mouthed teachers. I'm sorry for the children here. Heartily sorry.'

The woman was on her feet. Her chins were trembling. She pointed a finely manicured finger at Paulie. 'Out! Get out. Get out of my school. That note might have been written by an illiterate as you say but whoever he or she is, they are a moral person. Which is more than I can say for you.'

Paulie backed out and banged the door behind her. She had felt cool inside the room, but now she was trembling. 'Stupid,' she said to herself. 'What have you done to yourself now, Paulie?'

'Excuse me… Excuse me!' In the white van Paulie was dragged back to the present by a little voice in the cubicle on her left in the van. 'Excuse me?'

She stretched upwards but she could not manage to see her neighbour. 'Yes, what is it?' she said.

'Could you just let that woman out there know I want to go to the toilet?' It was the smelly old woman who had got on the van in front of her. She had quite a refined voice for someone who smelled so high.

'What?'

'I'm afraid I really do need to go to toilet. Can you let that young woman know? The one in the uniform?'

'I don't know…'

'Just beside your door,' called Christine from the other side. 'A button… Press it.'

Paulie found the button with a peeling notice

underneath it saying 'Only to be pressed in dire emergency.' She pressed it.

An intercom buzzed. 'What is it?'

'The old lady. She wants to go to the lav.'

'She'll have to put a cork in it. We can't stop now. We're only five minutes from the gate.' The intercom crackled off.

There was a silence. Then Queenie sighed. 'Oh dear,' she said. 'It'll have to come. Such a shame.'

'Oh dear!' said Paulie.

'Oh dear!' said Christine.

'Oh dear!' said Maritza.

And as the van filled with the choking stink they broke into laughter, laughter sharply edged with hysteria. Even Queenie chuckled.

The only person who didn't laugh was Lilah, who was sitting rigid with her temple on the steel partition, thinking that dying must be easier than having to bear this pain.

20 THE CONTAINMENT OF WOMEN

Paulie: So, six years after meeting those women on the van here I am, on the out, sitting in the hotel reception, my new, neatly packed baggage at my feet, when the double doors bursts open and a woman in battered jeans with a baby on her hip falls through the door. Her eye falls on me. 'Paulie?' she says.

I stand up awkwardly. 'Yes?'

She shakes my hand, and then changes the baby to the other hip. She smells of cinnamon. 'Fiona, John Kebler's wife,' she smiles. 'He sent me for you…'

Sent her?

'Apologies from him. University crisis. Come on, come on! I'm on a yellow line.'

So I'm bundled into a car - smelling of oranges and baby milk - whose door needs three bangs to close properly. The woman straps the baby into a seat at the back, jumps in beside me and revs the engine up so fast the car leaps like a cat off its brakes. Now she is twisting her body, stretching forwards and backwards to see her way at the junction before I bring a word into my mouth.

'Pleased to meet you Fiona,' I say. I suppose there must be irony in my tone, because she casts me a wild glance and grins. Her lipstick has only survived on the edges of her lips and her hair is uncombed. The hands gripping the steering wheel are unwashed, 'Oh. Was I brusque? So sorry. Afraid I have a lot on.'

'I could have got a taxi, Fiona. If John had telephoned. Given me the address. No need for you to come.'

'Nonsense. Wouldn't think of it. Waste of money.' Her voice has that velvet tone and cut-glass edge that's impossible to imitate without caricature. I've heard it on the radio but have only heard it once before in the flesh. That was a deputy Governor of a prison in the Midlands. That one had been to Roedene and Oxford and had an outsize social conscience. It would have been very satisfying if she'd been a rubbish officer. But she wasn't bad, got a lot of respect.

The road ahead is quieter now. We're out of the city centre, moving through tall brick houses with narrow gardens at the front. Some of these are full of dusty privet and old prams. Some are miniature cottage gardens.

'John told me about you,' she says, turning down yet another avenue.

'Has he, now?'

'It was very unfair, all that business. Grossly unfair.'

'Yeah. I've been thinking that for six years.'

A peal of laughter. 'You're right Paulie. Words are pretty stupid, aren't they?' She pulls up in front of this house which is double fronted and has a gravel garden in front, with rather tired rose bushes set into it.

I take a deep breath. 'Is this it?' I say. 'What's their name?'

'Kebler,' she says. 'We live here.' She gets out and leans to unstrap the baby. 'Come on, Paulie, the boot's open.'

'Kebler? Your house? I can't stay here.'

'That's what John said. I persuaded him otherwise.' She jumps out and unstraps the baby.

Now I'm angry as I pull my bags out of the boot. Trapped! Trapped into a favour that I do not want. I've had six years of that. Go here, go there, do as you're told. For your own good.

'Come on, Paulie,' she urges. The baby on her arm, she's already unlocking the door. The house smells of cooking; tomatoes and onions. Garlic. Should I feel surprised? The hall is cluttered with bikes and baby buggies. On the rail underneath the stairs there's a tide of coats and hats, wellingtons and battered cardboard boxes. An open door on my right reveals more clutter and the closed door on my left with a brass plate on saying John Kebler, FRCP.

Now John Kebler's wife is striding through to the back, leading me into a huge kitchen - this must be three rooms opened up into one. It has a long table down the middle, a battered sofa at one end and open shelves around a very big cooker which looks like a café cooker I saw once in a 1940s film. She puts the baby on the floor and throws herself onto the couch. 'Home sweet home!' she grins up at me. 'Welcome, Paulie.'

I keep my arms close to my sides and look down at her, miserably. 'I can't stay here Fiona. I have things to do. I've just come away from being monitored twenty four hours a day. I want no more of that. Honestly, I'd be better off in a squat.'

She leaps to her feet again. 'Here? Not *here*, Paulie. You won't be *here*.' She glances at the baby, and then picks it up. It's all baggy sweatshirt and leggings and bald head. I can't tell whether it is a girl or boy. A bit of John Kebler in this bundle. A bit of this girl Fiona. She leads the way out of the back door and we go down two steps and open another door. 'This belonged to John's daughter, my stepdaughter. Kind of snug bedsitter, I suppose. She's off to America this year doing some potty archeology in the badlands.'

The room's all right. Couch bed. Corner kitchen. Three lamps. Even a radio. 'There's a shower and loo through that door, Paulie. But if you want a bath you'd have to come upstairs.' She opens the curtains. The window has bars.. Now that's ironic. 'This is the front of the house. You can watch people's legs as they pass by.'

'Won't she mind? John's daughter?'

'Mind? My dear, she'll be too busy flapping her fabulous lashes at gorgeous diggers to give a damn.' She pauses. 'She gets them from John. Wonderful lashes.'

I only just stop myself saying I'd noticed that. 'Well, all right. I'll stay till ... I get myself sorted.' I feel miserable.

She sobers a little. The fizzing humour goes out of her. 'Don't worry about it, Paulie. Somebody owes you something, for goodness' sake.' The baby on her hip starts to whimper. 'Now then, get yourself unpacked, move the room about to suit you, make yourself at home. Then you can pop upstairs and raid my larder.'

'Is there a shop close by?'

'In the next street. Used to be a decent grocer's, but now it's all *chi chi*. Sweet potatoes and sun-dried tomatoes and that rubbish.'

'Well, I'll stock up there. I do have some money, you know.'

Her gaze rests on me, neutral as washed grey socks. 'Indeed you do. And more to come, I hope. So shop for yourself Paulie if you want. Just climb the steps to the street. No need to come through the house at all, unless you want to.' It's hard to tell, from that cut-glass voice whether or not she's offended. Perhaps she's pleased that I want to stay so separate. But as the door clicks to behind her I couldn't care less.

I look around at what is, at least for the time being, my own space. I unpack the stuff from the bag, and then take my rucksack to the shop to buy my own food, already exulting in the choices I can make.

Back in the room, I make myself tea, lie down on the divan and fiddle with the radio till I find music. I only drink half the cup and I have to lie back on the bed, my eyes drooping. I am too exhausted even to hold the cup. It's far too tiring, this living on the out. Too tiring altogether.

In the introduction to her book of poems called *Containment*, written while in prison, Paulie Smith wrote of the place where the five women first met:

'... *Brontë House was a small women's prison on the edge of a city in the North. Twenty five years old, the place was comparatively new: 'humanely' designed in red brick and strong cream paint. There were rumours of new extensions because (in those years) so many more women were ending up behind bars. The house was dedicated for the containment of women, women on short sentences and those on remand.*

As a consequence, Brontë House was filled with the sense of being on the edge. Women had just come in, or were just going out. They were seeing their briefs, desperately trying to 'get the depositions right', as though their own freedom depended on this turn of a phrase. They were waiting for a visit from their children or just recovering from one. They were under the blanket, enduring Cold Turkey from drugs. Or - having got clean in their time there - thinking about how on the out, they'd try just one more hit. Some women were putting in apps or applications: to change their cell or their cell-mate; to see Probation; to get clothes out of their stock in Reception; to object to unfair comments on their files.

The women were confronted with cell-mates who were — variously - predatory, depressed, non-stop talkers, self-harmers, mad, unclean, or given to snoring in the night. They were dealing with doctors and nurses, some of whom still thought they were in the nineteenth century workhouse. They were dealing with officers who had their own peculiarities, their own agendas, even when they were comparatively benevolent, kind, and good at their jobs. Not all of them were like that, of course.

So everyone at Brontë House - staff and inmates alike — lived on the edge. They operated on a basis of uncertainty, the fragile filaments of which kept the place running and held it together as it delivered up again - more or less intact - human beings for judgment, punishment or release…'   P.Smith

21 A COOL RECEPTION

In the waiting space at Reception, Queenie Pickering was crying - blubbing like a baby. The long shower they'd made her take had been very painful. Maritza found herself touching the old woman, stroking her arm.   She was wearing rough towelling robe, that - over- washed and discoloured - was the twin of the one Maritza herself had been allotted.   'Don't worry, Queenie.   Don't worry. It'll…'   She couldn't tell her it would be all right.   She didn't know that. None of them knew that. 'Shsh,' she said. 'Shsh.'

They'd taken away Queenie's bag and burnt it and its contents.   They'd taken her hat, of course.   They'd taken her clothes and burnt them too.   Even her armour-like brassiere and her large badly stained pants were burnt. She was allowed to keep her battered leather purse which had photos in it. One was of herself with her mother and father; a pretty girl, a man with a stiff winged collar and a woman with a collapsed face that had once been good looking. The other photograph was of a pretty young woman with wavy hair wearing a neatly belted print dress: a young teacher with her first class of seven year olds.

The other women from the van had to bag up their possessions and leave them in Reception. Before being given the towelling robes,   they'd all been surveyed like dogs at a dog show. They were examined under their hair, under their armpits, between their legs. The officer whose job it was - a sturdy woman with dyed blonde hair - caught Paulie's look. 'We have to do it, love. Drugs! Bring them in all ways, they do. In the bairn's nappies on visiting day. French kissing their boyfriends when they leave. Mouth to mouth supply.' She glanced across at Lilah who was sitting on the bench shivering, staring straight ahead of her. 'So desperate they are, poor buggers'll do anything.'

She proceeded very carefully to poke at the bandages on Christine's arms. Christine winced. The officer shook her head. 'There's nowt there but bloody arms, is there love?' She glanced again at Paulie. 'Need to check, love. More than my job's worth to leave it.' She patted the bandage back in place and Christine winced again.

Maritza leaned across and whispered to Christine. 'That looks nasty, your arm.'

Christine glanced at the other woman her eyes narrow. She had a nice little haircut. Clean fingernails. Even in the squalid prison wrap she looked out of place. 'It's gettin' better now,' she said, trying to breathe evenly.

A second officer, taller and thinner, called from the doorway. 'Get a move on, will you? Only ten minutes to feeding.' They used the word feeding in the prison, as though it were a farm.

Every single thing about them was entered in a book. *Height. Weight. Hair colour. Tattoos.* The marks on Christine's arm. Maritza saw the officers exchange glances at the sight of this mess.

Then they were allowed to dress again in their own clothes. The tall officer gave Queenie a pile of faded but clean clothes. Brassiere, knickers, tracksuit, socks and cotton plimsolls. The old woman cried louder at this. 'But these are men's clothes! I can't wear men's clothes.'

The officer shook her head. 'All we've got love. You can get someone to send something in.'

Suddenly they were all, even Lilah, looking at the hunched scarecrow figure of the old woman. Queenie sniffed, then her head went up. 'I had everything I needed, dear. It was all in my bags. But they took them away for the incinerator, they said. Even my hat! My scarves. And, dear, there is no 'someone' to send in some more things for me.' Tears were falling down the dried up furrows of her cheeks.

Then they were allocated their places. Paulie found herself in a cell with Queenie; Maritza was with Christine. Lilah was put in an observation cell on her own.

'Phew, that's a relief,' said Christine as she leapt on the top bunk and left the bottom bunk for Maritza.

'Relief? What?' said Maritza wearily, looking around the drab cell which was not clean but not dirty, and where the brightest colour was dun, the brightest light the dull shine on the steel toilet and washbasin.

'Not getting in with the junkie, that's what.'

'The girl with the long hair? Poor thing.'

'Coupla weeks torment she's in for. Under the blanket. You can be sorry for her but you don't wanter be on the bottom bunk, love, when she's doing her moaning and groaning, you believe me.' Christine sat with her back to the wall, legs dangling over the edge. 'You got people on the out?' she said.

Maritza, sitting on a chair by the window looked up at her. 'Yes. Two boys, Rory and Sam.'

'In care, are they?'

'No. With my mother, actually.'

143

'Actually? Get you! Actually I was in care myself.'

Maritza's heart sank at the tone. 'My mother offered to take care of them. We don't really get on, you know, me and my mother. So it was good of her to offer.'

Christine laughed: a hard chipped-ice sound. 'My mother can't stand me. Thinks I'm the devil's spawn.'

Maritza was spared the need to answer as, with a jangling of keys and a turning of locks, an officer opened the door. 'Dinner, girls,' he said cheerfully. 'Settling in, are we?'

Maritza sat up straight, as a woman, obviously another prisoner, passed in their plastic trays with their plastic forks and plastic plates. Their first meal was in their cells.

'All pals are yeh?' The man looked bright-eyed from one to the other. 'Palsie walsie.' He laughed. 'Why, yer'd better be. Yer'll be eatin' together, pissin' together and cryin' together – from now on.'

Maritza's heart lurched. This was real. It was all real. It was real as cabbages. Christine waited till the door clicked behind him and grunted. 'Wanker,' she said. 'This business is full of wankers, both sides of the door.'

Maritza looked up at the younger girl, placidly eating the piled up potato and beans. 'Doesn't it bother you all this? I was terrified ... I am frightened.'

'One, don't be scared darlin'. Being scared shows too much. Lets them in. Gives the wankers too much fun.' Christine winked. 'Two, don't think it's like on the telly, all those dykes and staff with attitude. Stop worrying your little head about that. It's not as interesting as that. It's routine, blank routine. Not enough to do. Too much time to think. If you're lucky you'll sleep a lot. Me. I can't sleep. I stay

144

awake and think of killing my mother.'

Maritza drew in a breath and put her tray on the floor, her dinner uneaten. Christine laughed, still munching. 'Don't worry about me darlin'. I've been thinking about that since I was twelve. It's my hobby. My other hobby is drinking vodka and beating up on policemen. You not eating that?' She nodded towards Maritza's still full plate.

Maritza handed it up to her and lay back on her bunk, closed her eyes and tried to think of nothing. A sudden warmth swept towards her. She opened her eyes. Christine's head appeared over the edge of the bunk. 'Maritza?'

'Yes.'

'Where d'you get a name like that? Sounds like a chocolate bar.'

Maritza yawned. 'My mother. It was from an operetta. She used to like operetta.'

'Operetta? My God! What've we come to? Fucking operetta.' Christine groaned. 'Tell you what, we'll call yer Ritzy. Much better.'

'Sounds like a gangster's moll,' said Maritza.

'Yeah, like I said, much better innit?'

Then a high pitched buzzer sounded outside, and they could hear a voice shouting, swearing. Maritza sat up and cracked her head on the bunk above. 'What's that?' she said, her scalp crawling.

'That'll be the junkie. She'll be a stranger to herself for weeks yet. And they'll give her nothing. Nothing for the pain. The doc says it's not pain. Just your fuckin' body getting rid of the toxins. Tell that to a junkie.

22 FROM THE CORNER OF MY EYE

Two cells away Queenie, tears all dried, was tucking into her dinner with relish. 'Ah, this is nice,' she said. 'Do you know it's quite a while since I had a meal?'

Paulie ploughed through the heap of food, chewing every mouthful very slowly. She looked round the room. Small shelf. Plastic mirror. Notice board. No drawing pins but patches of white powder where pictures had been stuck with toothpaste. In the corner there was a postcard picture of boats clicking together in a Cornish harbour. A cruel image in here, where the most you could see was the tree in the yard and the cells on the other side of the square. In here the scenery consisted of the steel basin and the toilet beside it. She looked down at Queenie. God! Going to the toilet in the same room as that old tramp woman. Or anyone. Even at the squat she'd repaired the bolt on the toilet door so it worked. Charlie had laughed at her over that. Called her a prude, frightened of her own nature. Tears filled her eyes and started to plop onto her plate.

'Will you be wanting that?' Queenie had stood up from the bottom bunk and was standing, her face level with Paulie's knees.

Paulie looked down at the plate, the food only half-eaten. 'No. Do you want it?'

'If you don't mind. Do you know, suddenly I feel all right? It's safe in here. Not cold. Do you think He'll be able to get in here?'

'Who?'

'Him. The Devil. No, I don't really think so. Forty-foot wing span! That'll give Him a problem. Could never get through those windows, could he?'

Paulie looked down at the old women and thrust the plastic plate towards her. 'Here! You might as well finish this off. I'm not hungry.'

Queenie took it, eyes sparkling and Paulie lay back on the bunk and rolled over so she was looking at the wall. Charlie had been furious at her walking out on her job. 'That's it, then. Us up the Khyber Pass without a paddle.'

'What? The Khyber Pass? Charlie...'

'Shut up.' He turned his back on her.

She'd sat on the couch, her head spinning, staring at his back. Suddenly, against all her rules, she *did* want his support, his help, his reassurance. She wanted him to put his arms round her and say it was OK, that he would take care of her, and that they would cope together. She had coped since she was twelve when her father had started his downward slide. Now she just wanted to give in, to be comforted by someone who cared.

Then he had turned back towards her, his face beaming. She went towards him. 'I've got it!' he said. 'I've fuckin got it.'

'What?' She was in his arms. It felt very warm in there.

'You can go on the graft.'

She pulled away. 'What?' she said bleakly.

'Well, you can't do the money machines. You'd stick out like a sore thumb, no street bunny, you. But, togged up like a teacher, you can do the big stores. Jeans.

Appliances! You graft'em and I'll shift them. There's a pub - The Green Bell. The woman there'll give you a list. Graft to order, no waste... Hey, what's the matter?'

She was feet away from him now. 'What am I to you, Charlie? What am I?'

He shrugged. 'You're my ... well, my girlfriend.'

'Meal ticket? Is that what I've been?'

He dropped his gaze. 'Whatever,' he said. 'I liked you.'

'Maybe not as much as the stuff you're putting up your nose, in your arm, now.'

He put a hand out to her. 'Paulie, I really liked you. Independent. The stand-alone woman. A bloke gets enough of snivelling babes. I liked you.'

She noticed, not for the first time, the shadows under the eyes in that beautiful face. She sat back on the couch. 'Can you get that list?' she said.

'List?'

'The list from the pub.'

He grinned, came to sit beside her. 'I can get it, kiddo. I can get it. And I can show you the ropes in the stores. Though I can't graft myself; they know me, see?'

'Don't worry about me, Charlie. I know the ropes.'

'You know the ropes?' He stared at her.

'Baby, I was shoplifting while you were still in nappies. Retired undefeated when I was sixteen.'

He was interested. 'Why d'you stop, Paulie?'

She wrinkled her nose at him. 'That's for me to know and you to find out.' For a long second in her nostrils was the stench of the room where her father died. She could see the pile of grey ashes scattered over his chair. 'Now then, Charlie. How d'we get this list?'

he clink of keys and the heavy rattle on the door pulled Paulie back again to the present.

'Plates! Caff's closed!' The grinning face of the officer appeared at the door. Queenie had not finished devouring Paulie's dinner. 'Come on, Ma! Eat up.'

'I'm not finished, I'm afraid.'

'I'm not finished, I'm afraid, *sir*! ' The grin hardened on his face. 'You'd better get it right, Ma. Didn't they tell you in Reception? *Sir* and *Miss*. You get points off if you forget.'

Queenie started to cry. Paulie jumped down from the top bunk and took the plate from her. She gave it to the woman standing by the officer. 'She's finished, *sir*,' she said. 'I'm afraid she's a bit of a slow eater.'

He looked her up and down. 'Smith, is it?'

'Yes.'

'Yes, *sir*.'

'Yes, *sir*.' She smiled at him and his gaze dropped first. He clashed the door to and the keys ground in the lock.

Queenie was sniffing, rubbing her face with the back of her hand.

'Don't worry about him, Queenie. Wanker just fancies himself. It's his fun. Nothing to worry about.'

The old woman gave her a watery smile. 'Miss. Sir? That's what they said in that other room. That room where they took my clothes and my hat. Call them Miss and Sir, they said, I have to call them Miss and Sir. Those young men, those young women!'

'It's just their rules, Queenie. They like to keep their rules.'

Queenie nodded. 'Oh, I know about rules. I used to say to my children rules are the framework for civilisation.'

'Children?'

Queenie smiled at her. 'They used to call me Miss. Called me Miss for forty years, my dear.'

A thrill of shock rippled through Paulie from her heels to her forehead. 'You were a teacher?'

Queenie nodded with satisfaction. 'The same village school. They called me Miss there for forty years.'

'Me too.'

Queenie frowned at her. 'You? In the village? I never saw you.'

'I was a teacher too. They called me Miss, but it seemed very strange. Just for a year, though. Not forty years.'

Queenie laughed. 'But you're just a child yourself...'

'I was a teacher, for ... well ... about a year, like I say.'

'Well I never.' Queenie got up and went to sit on the single chair beside the barred window. 'They don't like it when you run away, you know. I ran away once.'

'From a prison?'

Queenie shook her head. 'From a hospital. I don't like those places. Don't like them. They give you stuff so you sleep or bump against the furniture.'

'Why do they do that?'

'Because they don't want me to see what I see. The old Devil and the Water Man with the fairies dancing at his shoulder. Then I see the leaves moving and growing. Moving around, closing in on you. And the trees that touch heaven. I see my father and my mother, although in this place my mother has all her teeth. And the trees standing up on their hind legs and walking across the land. Of course that upset the people in the hospital. They just wanted me to see fog and furred up windows.'

'How long did you see all this? All those things?' said Paulie. 'The Water Man …'

'Well, d'you see, I'd always seen them, through the corner of my eyes. Since I was a little girl. They were always there, waiting. But I had school and college. I was very busy. My dear mother wanted me to do well. I tried to work hard just for her. Then, they died - he and she - in a month. My mother and father. Did I tell you she had no teeth?

Then I was so busy with the children in the school, you see, and keeping the school house clean. So many ants in there, dear. So many wasps. But then, when the school closed down altogether and the children went to school in the next village, I finally had time: time for them, the Great Ones of the forest could at last make their way to the centre of my life. Sometimes they ran away into the woods and I had to seek them out. We had some lovely times together dear.

But it upset people, me at night searching the woodland. First they made fun of me. Then I had to go to hospital. Lots of fogs and furred up windows after that, of course.'

Paulie closed her eyes. A crazy woman! Locked up twenty-two hours a day with a woman who was clearly, if benevolently, insane. She wanted to laugh. She wanted to cry. She didn't know what she wanted to do

23 UNDER THE BLANKET

The officer lifted the blanket from Lilah's face. 'You all right in there? You pressed the button?'

Lilah gritted her teeth. 'I told you I wanted to see a doctor.'

'Like I told you before, love, they'll see to you in the morning. There'll be a surgery in the morning.'

'I'm dying here. I'm telling you,' she mumbled.

'No you're not. You just think you're dying.' The door creaked shut. The keys ground in the lock. She could hear them jangling on the woman's thigh as she walked back along the corridor.

Lilah pulled the blanket back over her head and curled up again. In the end, with her and Jonno, each day had resolved itself into an iron-clad routine. You got up, feeling lousy, drank coffee and smoked cigarettes to pull you round. Sorted the sitting room and kitchen from the night before. Jonno always needed a fix to pull him round for the day. If they had gear there might be a few callers. Jonno might go and get some chips from the shop. They would count their money. If there was enough Jonno would put it in an envelope for her and make her repeat three times what they wanted. Then she would drive to the town fourteen miles distance to get new supplies from a man they knew there, whose prices were right.

Jonno had stopped going out. By early afternoon he was too stoned to drive; usually asleep. By the time she got back with the gear he would be in the kitchen, stoking himself up with coffee. They would lay out the gear on the table, cut it and split it up into wraps. Plenty of wraps there to sell on, plenty for themselves. The one funded the other. They worked this routine day by day. By midnight, they and whoever else was in the house, were stoned. And the next day it all started all over again.

Now, in the cell Lilah turned over and stretched out to ease her leg a bit, then curled up in a small ball, very tightly, to make herself a smaller target for the black, oily, aching universe that was surging towards her again. The pain was unbearable. She screamed, but no-one came.

24 THE BEAST

Christine lay back in the eternal dusk of the cell. It was never truly dark in prison. How many hours till morning? The muttering on the corridor had faded almost to nothing. The tannoy radio was turned off. The doors had stopped clashing. Around them the whole building seemed to hum with presence - so many people breathing the hot dusty air in and the same number breathing the hot dusty air out. She started to choke.

She jumped down from the top bunk and peered out into the yard. She wedged the narrow window open. The night outside was dry and cool. She breathed the air in. Breathed the air out. Deal with it. Deal with it. She knew how to deal with it. One of those fancy counsellors had told her about the breathing. Sometimes it was a help. Sometimes she was beyond the breathing, quite beyond it. She pulled at her bandage and winced, not unhappy to feel the pain.

'Did you do it yourself? That thing on your arm?' The voice came from the darkness of the bottom bunk.

'Mind your own fucking business.' She leaned across to Maritza's shelf. 'Fluffy toy?' She picked up the black and white panda. 'A few of the lasses have fluffy toys, but I wouldn't'a thought you were the type.'

Maritza stared at the panda, almost invisible in the prison dusk. The toy was the first thing she'd put in the little bag she was allowed to bring in here.

'Does that thing belong to one of your kids?' Christine's voice floated down.

'No,' said Maritza slowly. 'I had a panda when I was little and I lost it. And I got myself one a year or so back. It's a kind of mascot.'

Christine put it back carefully on the shelf. 'A mascot,' she said. 'Yes.'

Out in the yard a voice roared into the darkness.

'There they go!' said Christine.

Maritza sat up and cracked her head again. 'Ouch. What is it?'

'Listen!' said Christine.

The women in the place started to each other cross the open space between the blocks. They called people by name, asking about people from other places, reminiscing about other jails. They shouted to each other about sentences they were serving, or would get. About men. About children and changing partners. About what the men should have done to them. About scoring money and drugs on the out. All this was conducted at the level of a roar laced with the foulest language Maritza had heard in her life. (The Frog Woman, in whose house she lived after her father died, had washed Maritza's mouth out with soap when she'd talked once about a damned lad who had tripped her up on her way back from school.)

She sat forward to hear more clearly. The shouting had taken on another, more urgent note. Her blood froze. The target for the shouting now moved to herself and the women from the van. 'Hey! Chickens! Fuckin' new lasses today, eh! Down in the van. How d'yah like the paddy wagon, hey?'

'Are you fuckin' there, are you chickens?'

'Ye've come to the right place here, haven't they lasses? Best fuckin' prison in England!'

'Pin you down and fuck you rotten in this place!' The voices were coming out of the dark in great hoarse billows of sound. It was hard to believe they came out of the mouths of human beings.

'So what they call yer? Tell us yer names. Them lasses in E5. What they call yer?'

('Stay quiet, Christine's voice came down softly to Maritza out of the darkness. 'Stay quiet I tell yer!')

'So what they call yer, then?'

'What they fuckin' call yer?'

'E6 - what about E6? What they call yer?'

('Ignore them dear,' said Queenie to Paulie. 'Such bad manners, shouting like that.')

Paulie had jumped down from her bunk and was on her feet, straining, wondering whether to comply, to give them her name. It might be the friendly thing to do. She had to survive here. She opened her mouth.

Queenie pulled her arm. 'Don't say it,' she whispered. 'Remember the games you played in the playground? They ask you your name and you must not tell. You're in their power if you tell.'

'Well,' roared this voice of the yard. 'Give us a song then! Sing us a fuckin' song. Are ye fuckin' deaf or fuckin' daft?'

The compulsion to sing, to make some kind of communication into the void was almost overwhelming.

'Don't do it,' said Christine to Maritza.

'Don't do it,' said Queenie to Paulie.

Then, suddenly the voices faded and they were all

left in peace.

In their new cells the new prisoners settled back into their bunks and pulled up their blankets. Each of them closed their eyes and tried to get to sleep in their own way and survive until morning.

25 NOW, BEGINNING

'Paulie! Paulie!'

The keys. Where are the keys? I can't hear the keys. For a second my eyes won't open, my arms won't move. I must have been dreaming. I know it was a dream. I dreamt I was eating in a riverside pub with a very elegant woman who made a pass at me. And I was bathing in bubbles a foot high, in a room with white tiles edged with blue. 'Would you like a drink?' The woman is leaning towards me, her gaze benevolent. I notice now she has no clothes on and her breasts are dropping in two perfect arcs.

'Paulie! Paulie! Will you open this door?' A man's deep voice.

My eyes snap open properly to see a small room with a small lamp, with posters on the wall. I sit up. Yes. The daughter's room. I leap off the couch and I unlock my door. I unlock *my* door! Note this. *Unlock my own door.*

I open the door to the frowning face of John Kebler. 'Sorry,' I yawn. 'I just dropped off.'

Calmness drops onto him like a cloak. 'Paulie,' he smiles his hesitant smile. 'How is it? Have you settled in?'

'Yeah.' I step back so he can follow me into the room. 'It's cosy here. But...'

'But...?'

'Well you know I didn't want to be here. What wife would want a jailbird under her roof? Well ... under her feet.'

He sits down easily by the table. 'It's no trouble, Paulie. The room's empty. Anyway till September. And Fiona … well … she was as outraged at the deal you got as I was. You are not a jailbird.'

'She's all right, Fiona.'

He nods. 'Glad you think so. She says to come up for a drink at about nine. The baby'll be asleep by then, with luck.'

'I don't drink. I don't drink, I don't smoke. You know that.'

'Don't be awkward, Paulie. It's not necessary now.'

I wait. I don't want to have to ask the question about the woman from the van.

He goes for his pocket. 'Look. I've only turned up one address so far. Had to do it through people I knew, first Probation and then the Social Services. They had to ring her to see if she minded and it seems she doesn't.'

'Who?' I say, grabbing the paper. 'Who is it?' I put it under the lamp and read his spidery writing.

'Maritza Molloy,' he says. 'And that's her address. It's a big new housing development the other side of the river.'

'Only Maritza?'

He shakes his head. 'Greedy Paulie! I'll keep trying. But Maritza may know something about the others.' He stands up, almost blocking the light from the narrow window. 'Paulie?'

'Yes?'

'I'm not your psychiatrist any more. You know that?'

'You never were my psychiatrist,' I say. 'You were

theirs.'

'Well, anyway, it's OK to be friends now.' He puts out his hand and I cannot escape shaking it. I pull mine away fast.

He turns to the door, and then turns back. 'You've cut your hair,' he says. 'It suits you. Oh! Don't forget nine o'clock. Fiona's looking forward to it.'

The door shuts behind him and I lock it. Being here's all going to take some handling. I hope I'm up to it. But at least tomorrow's taken care of. Tomorrow. Tomorrow! I'm going to see Maritza Molloy.

26 HAIR

It took seventeen days at Brontë house for Lilah to wake up with no pain, just the dull ache of exhaustion and, even more strangely, the scrape of hunger in her stomach. She was suddenly ravenously hungry. Even the starchy basic prison food tasted good. Sometimes she would remember the physical pain of the last weeks and shudder inwardly. She still suffered overwhelming cramps but the first nightmare did not return with full force, all guns blazing.

She was offered some weed on the exercise yard but she managed turned it down. 'How d'you get it in here?' she asked the girl.

The girl winked. 'It gets in. Not enough of it, but it gets in.'

'What about brown?' said Lilah. She told herself she was only curious. But really she was very scared. Her gut wanted the hit, for the relief, for the healing. But she, Lilah, whose gut it was, didn't want to touch that stuff again

The girl shook her head. 'No chance love. My lad says they can get that in the men's jail, but not here. You won't get that much here.'

An officer on the wing encouraged Lilah to go to the classroom, and she went, glad of something to do. She went over simple sums and English exercises which was easy and soothing. She took her first steps on a long.

The old lady was usually in the classroom; the tramp - woman who had caused the bother in the van. Lilah had been dimly aware of that, even through the maze. The old woman sat at a table doing a very elaborate word puzzle, which seemed to be going on day after day. The other women from the van were in the classroom too. There was the tall, hefty girl who cut her arms. The little one with short hair who looked like a librarian. And the fresh faced one with the keen face and the punk haircut.

Paulie looked up and caught her glance and held it. 'Feelin' better, are you?' she said.

Lilah nodded. 'Still get the aches. Flashbacks too. But I'm getting there.'

Paulie shook her head. 'Must be a nightmare.'

'You done it? Have you turkeyed like that?'

Paulie shook her head. 'No. My boyfriend was a user. Spent half his time between here and eternity.' She bit her tongue. Perhaps she shouldn't say anything. Young Christine said you shouldn't say anything.

'But *you* don't?'

Paulie shook her head. 'I did use a bit when I was young, but never after that. I just stopped. Never will again. Mug's game. Never had to turkey. Even then.'

'Lucky you!' said Lilah. 'That's me, though. Never again. I'll never do any of that again.'

'You'll be lucky,' piped up Christine from the other side of the classroom. 'You know what they say, once a junkie, always a junkie.' Tension, expectancy rippled through the whole room. There was some relish in the thought of a fight. The girls put down their pens and watched.

'What do you know?' Lilah lunged for her, but Paulie pulled her back. The teacher, sitting at the front desk, looked up and watched carefully as the situation settled itself.

'Take no notice,' said Paulie. 'Leave it.'

Lilah caught up with Christine as they were being led back to their cells before dinner. 'No need to mouth off like that, in front of everyone," she said. 'Not called for.'

Christine eyed her, then shrugged. 'No harm meant darlin'. You get bored sometimes, just breaks it up a bit.'

'Watch it, then! I'm tellin' yer.'

Christine peeled off into her cell, followed by the mousy librarian woman, who nodded at Lilah. 'Good to see you up and about,' she said. 'We were worried about you in the van.'

When Maritza got into the cell she said to Christine, 'That's a bit uncalled for. The girl's just through that turkey thing.' (Maritza was surprised how easy these new words came to her now.) Turkey. On the in. On the out.

Christine leapt onto the top bunk, making the metal framework rattle. 'So what?' she said. 'She needs to watch out. I've seen plenty come off it and be clean as a whistle, then as they get ready to go out, what're they looking forward to? Their first hit. She needs a warning.'

'For a second I thought she'd hit you.'

Christine laughed. 'I'd like to have seen her try,' she said thoughtfully. 'Or anyone else.'

That night, after tea, during Association, Lilah was allowed a long shower before coming back to the dining room to wait her turn for the hair dryer. The women were engrossed in their own chat, reading magazines, watching the chattering television, playing draughts. The women at her end of the room watched with some interest as she blew her long hair dry, watching it rise away from the dryer like lifted silk.   In the weeks when she was under the blanket Lilah had left her hair in its disfiguring plait. No one had ever seen it brushed out.

'What beautiful hair you have, dear,' said Queenie. 'D'you know,' she said to Paulie, 'My own mother had hair long enough to sit on. Just like that. But she wore it braided round her head like a long ribbon.'

Another girl took Lilah's place with the hairdryer and Lilah came to sit beside Paulie and began to comb her hair with her small comb. Christine called across the table. 'I'll plait it for you if you like,' she said. 'I used to do it once for a black lass in one place I was in.   She had fabulous hair, that lass. Very thick and very fine.'

Lilah stared at her.

'It'll stay in for a week. More. ' said Christine.

'OK.'

Christine nodded with satisfaction. 'Right. Sit here.' A few of the women crowded round and watched. Christine only managed two long, thin plaits before it was the end of Association.   They all groaned.

'Give us a bit longer, sir,' said Christine. 'I've not finished this plait yet.'

'Get yerself down here, Cazelet,' said the man. 'Association over, you know the rules.'

In each of the next six Associations Christine did a few more plaits for Lilah.   At the end of that time Lilah had a full head of plaited locks.   When Christine tied the last one off with a bit of wool, a cheer went round the room. 'Keen!' 'All right!' 'Cool!'

Then the officers started to bustle around. Clearly Association was cut short because they were wary that too much joy could lead to trouble.

Lilah's pad mate (the third in three weeks, so fast did they move through) approved of the effect. 'You can even wash them like that, you know,' she said admiringly. 'I knew a girl in Holloway who had her locks in for three months.'

Hair was also the topic of discussion two cells down. 'Your hair's growing nicely too, dear,' said Queenie from her bottom bunk.

Paulie peered into the milky plastic mirror at her thickening thatch. 'So it is.'

'Do you know I thought you were a boy, when I first saw you?'

'A boy?'

'Your hair cut up at the back and sides like that. I had a boy in my very first class, Joseph Tye. He used to have hair like that. His father used to take the clippers right over his head. The others used to laugh at him. 1960 that was. They were growing their hair longer then.'

'They call that a Number One nowadays - quite the fashion. I liked mine short,' said Paulie, pushing her fingers through her hair and making it stand up all over her head. 'I like it.'Charlie used to like it too. 'My boyfriend used to like it,' she said. 'And he had long hair. Golden curls down to his shoulders.'

'Ah. The poet Byron,' said Queenie. 'He had golden curls. I have spoken to him you know! Long curls. A wonderful twinkle in his eye. He used to walk with me in the woodland. Near the village. By the edge of a long wall. Did I tell you about the village, dear, I...'

Paulie dropped on her knees beside Queenie's bunk.

'Queenie,' she said desperately. 'You shouldn't be in here. I'm gonna talk to somebody. The officers. Probation. The governor. You shouldn't be in here, you know. There are better places...'

Queenie's small hand shot out and grasped her arm in a vice-like grip. 'No. No, child. Don't do this. They'll put me in a hospital and who knows when they'll let me out? No, love, I'll stay for the three months and get out again.'

'But then, that's the street. You'd be back on the street.'

'The Probation lady talks about a flat.'

'Would you stay there?'

'Well, dear, we'd have to see, wouldn't we?'

Paulie sighed. 'Queenie, do you mind if I ask you something?'

Queenie patted her hand. 'No, dear. Anything.'

'Why on earth are you in here? Why on earth is a person like you in here?'

'Well, dear,' said Queenie brightly. 'I have two unfortunate tendencies. One of which is the tendency to run off to get lost when people crowd in on me. The other is a tendency to lash out and break things when very, very pressed.'

'So what did you do? Why are you here?'

'Well, it's quite a long story. I was in this shop and the owner was trying to shoo me away as though I were a dog. So, I'm afraid I winged him a bit with one of my bags, and then toppled a pile of KitKat and some very precariously balanced boxes of cereal. To be honest, just as he shouted, I saw the Winged One behind him and it was He at whom I lashed. Well, dear, they put me on probation for that but I ran off so I wouldn't have to see the probation man, who had rather an unfortunate moustache. Then they caught me and again I lashed out and the poor policeman lost his hat. Well, dear, the judge said I really should go to hospital…'

'So you should,' said Paulie feelingly.

'But there were no places in the hospital,' said Queenie with satisfaction. 'So I came here, which is not a bad place at all. Such nice young people.' She fiddled with her wallet. 'I wonder dear if you'd be kind enough to stick this photo on the board with your toothpaste – such a good idea, that.'

Paulie looked at the photo. 'This is you and your class?'

Queenie smiled her gap-toothed smile. 'My very first.' She pointed to a boy in the back row. 'He's a barrister now. He never could keep his workbook clean. All black fingermarks.' She pointed to a girl in the front row. 'And she has a very important post in the government. Always so neat. Such bright eyes.'

Paulie stuck it on the board with dabs of toothpaste thinking of the young teacher at the back of the cluster of children who also had very bright eyes.'

'You made a good job of Lilah's hair,' said Maritza. 'I think she liked it.' She was sticking photos of the boys on her pin board with dabs of toothpaste.

Christine, sitting on the chair with her feet up on the windowsill, said, 'That's all right then. Fair's fair, in your little world Ritzy.' Her head on one side, she surveyed her pad mate. 'Your own cushy little haircut's growing out, mind.'

Maritza put her head on one side and reached for her comb. 'Hasn't it? It's a mess. And I've got the boys coming to see me next week. They'll think I'm a hag. I look a mess.'

Christine looked harder. 'No you don't. Fact is, you look better'n when you came in.'

'Prison food. Junk food. Must have put on a stone.'

'Aye. Fills you out. That junkie must have put on half a stone in week. She has a good two stones to go, like.'

'Stop calling her a junkie.'

'If you say so.' Christine's feet came to the floor with a clash. 'Tell you what, Ritzy. I'll do your hair.'

Maritza laughed. 'Not enough here for plaits. Not for one plait.'

'Don't need'm. I've got some scrunchies here. Choose a colour.'

Maritza chose purple velvet, laughing. 'That's a Ritzy scrunchie I think. I don't know what you'll do. I might not like it.'

'You'll like it..' Christine sat her in the chair, and, wetting the comb under the tap of the sink, set about her work. She took Maritza's hair and combed it carefully over her hand. Then she pulled it back and up and tightened it inside the scrunchie. Then she pulled bits of hair down at the front and the sides and, spitting on her fingers, curled the hair round so it stayed. 'Problem with that good shop cutting,' she said. 'It takes the life out of your hair. Tames it.'

Maritza struggled under her hand. 'Let me see it,' she said.

'No, wait a sec.' Christine poked into her own precious stash of make-up and set about Maritza's face. 'There. You can look now.'

Maritza looked in the mirror, surveying Ritzy.

'You look ten years younger,' said Christine. 'Fifteen.'

Maritza laughed. 'So I do. I look like a ten years younger gangster's moll.'

'Yeah. Good isn't it? You look much better. A proper Ritzy.'

Maritza turned her face this way and that. 'It is an improvement. I like it.'

'Well, try it on your lads next week, won't you?'

Maritza, sobered, shook her head from side to side. 'Couldn't do that, Christine. It'd frighten them to death. It's too different. Not the Mum they know.'

Christine lay back on the bunk. 'Ask yourself! Were you the Mam they knew when you were the Mam they knew?'

Maritza sat on the chair and peered out into the darkening yard, the distant high fences with their razor wire on top. She'd looked forward to this first visit for a whole month. She'd written a letter every week to the boys. At first it was difficult to find anything to say. She didn't want to tell them about things in here: too bleak to write about. They really wouldn't understand. Then she discovered the Tuesday library in the prison, and deliberately read the kind of stories she knew they would like - adventure stories, science fiction. And in the letters she told them about the stories: the characters and the complicated the plot and the surprise at the end. And always she told them that she loved them and she always would.

Her mother had written a brisk letter saying the boys had settled in very well, considering. There was a stiff little letter from Sam with two kisses after his name. Nothing from Rory.

After writing her first few letters she started to read them out loud. She read them out to Christine, to see if they made sense to her, before she sealed them. Christine told her that the boys were lucky to have a mother like her and did she know it? 'Do you know, Ritzy, its weeks since I had that dream of killing my mother? A good sign, eh?'

'That's something.' Maritza knew enough now to be calm about this. Christine's arms had healed nicely and, apart from a few terrifying bouts of temper where she banged on the door till her knuckles came out in bruises, Christine had left her arms whole in the weeks in here.

'My sister's coming, you know,' said Christine into the darkness that night. 'She's coming on a visit, Ritzy.'

'Your sister?'

'Our Sallyanne. She's younger than me. Nineteen.'

'I didn't know you'd had a letter.' You couldn't have missed it, this close. Post was the highlight of the week. 'Did she write? Did you write?'

'I didn't. Probation told me. It's been fixed up.'

'How old is she, did you say?'

'Nineteen. Three years younger than me.'

'I didn't know you had a sister. You never said.'

'Nowt says you should know everything about me.'

'Yes. Yes. I suppose you're right.'

'Well, Ritzy, I do have a sister. Sallyanne. I haven't

seen her for three years.   Once I went to the house to see her but my mother chased me.'

'Wasn't that child's hair nice?' said Queenie, stretching first one foot in front of her, then another. 'She looked so nice in those plaits. So very neat, just think of her in the van! What a difference. Such lovely hair.' She sighed.

'We all look different, now,' said Paulie. 'Pasty-faced and fat. Hair all over the place.'

'I think your hair is very nice, dear. So thick, and now it's grown so nicely.' Queenie's tone would brook no opposition. Paulie had a glimpse of the placid, imaginative schoolmistress she must have been.

Paulie picked up her book. It was a novel by Ann Smiley, about the wide open spaces of America. She'd read three Ann Smileys this week and had booked two Toni Morrisons with the librarian.

'You read a lot, dear,' said Queenie.

'All there is to do.   In case you hadn't noticed Queenie, we're stuck in her twenty two hours in twenty four.'

'That's true, dear. I suppose I have my poetry to keep me occupied.' Queenie was trying to recite all the poems she knew - and she knew a lot - at least once every week.   Paulie listened to her declaim dozens of Browning poems and Yeats poems. As time went on learned them and joined in the recitation.   More than one officer had asked Paulie if it didn't get on her nerves, all that bloody chanting.   'It'd do my head in, all that fuckin' chantin'.' But it didn't do Paulie's head in. The continuous murmur was soothing, like some of those plain-song tapes Charlie had played once while he was gouching, lolling around full of drugs.

But even Paulie had to admit that she was unnerved by Queenie's shouts in the night, her overloud exhortation to the Water Man and the walking trees to guard the earth for her till she got back outside the walls. This made Paulie wish that she was padded up with a mouse type woman like Maritza.

She wondered what that Maritza was doing here. Not the type really. Not the type at all. And how did she manage with that explosive Christine? That temper. Bombastic wasn't in it. But even so Paulie thought Christine had something; some sparks that ten years in and out of institutions had not managed to extinguish. She was a bright spark in this drab place.

'I'm surprised, really,' Queenie's voice came at her through the darkness.

'What are you surprised at?'

'That you don't write things yourself Paulie. Clever girl like you. Poems. You could write some poems.'

Paulie laughed. 'Me? All those rhymes?'

'Oh no, dear. Didn't you know? Poems are not supposed to rhyme nowadays. It's against the rules. Even though the ones that rhymed are so much easier to learn.'

'Well ...' She hadn't thought of *writing*. Not at all. 'But...'

'Ask that nice teacher for some paper, dear. Do that.'

Paulie put down her book then picked it up again. No. She couldn't write poetry. Not her. Much later that night she felt Queenie stirring in the bottom bunk. 'Oh, I knew I was going to tell you something, dear. I forgot to mention.'

Paulie yawned. 'What is it Queenie?'

'How much I like perfume, I used to wear perfume all the time, dear. My one indulgence. My niece, Janine, brought it for me, off the plane. Air hostess, you know. On aeroplanes.'

'I didn't know you had a niece. You said you had no-one.'

'Well, she's really my second cousin's daughter. But she always called me auntie.' She paused, 'Rive Gauche and Je t'adore. They were my favourites.'

'Where is she, this niece?' Couldn't she send you some clothes?'

'Janine? Oh, no dear. She's in Canada, I believe. Sold my little house in the village and flew away. Such a nice girl. You would have liked her, Paulie.'

'Well,' thought Paulie, pulling the blanket over her head, 'Fuck Janine for a thieving little cow.'

27 PSYCHING FIRE

Five years after her release, in her acclaimed book *Behind the Door*, poet Paulie Smith was to write

'...The truth about what each woman had done, the truth about the life that led her to this place, would come out in spurts and trickles among the women. If it trickled out that a woman had anything to do with hurting children that woman suffered terrible sanctions. These did not always harm the flesh but sometimes seared the soul.

A certain modified degree of truth would occasionally emerge. How a woman's co-accused had got off on bail while she was in here taking the punishment for him; how the police would concoct evidence where they could not find it; how a girl had been rugby-tackled by a store detective and banged from unit to unit by him and his colleague. In this case there were photos that girl got off despite actually putting the silver figurine under her coat.

The people who knew most, if not all, of the stories of the women were the people who had the files: the people whose legitimate living was made out of the misery of these women. These were the professionals; the briefs and the psychs, probation officers social workers and prison officials.

It was with these people that the Brontë women needed to be the most open, the most guileful, the most persuasive, and the most poignant. With these people a woman had to present, or invent, a 'self' that was worth saving, she had to take herself beyond the level of merely being a case. Of course in some self-serving professionals quarters this might be labelled manipulative and that word would be added to the woman's file.'

The psych stood up from his chair and came forward to shake Paulie Smith's hand. 'Pauline is it? I'm John Kebler. Your solicitor Mr Callant would tell you I was coming to talk to you.'

She was back in Brontë House, the prison where she'd started five years ago. There were rumblings out there in the world about the safety of Paulie Smith's sentence. This psych's job was to inform with those rumblings.

She shook John Kebler's hand. 'Mr Callant said you were good at what you do.' She paused. 'If you're as good a psychiatrist as he's a solicitor, then I'm in the shit. He's missed three appointments out of four in the last month.' She sat down and looked at the psych across the table. 'If you're going to do word-association or show me inkblots like the last shrink did, you can get lost,' she said.

'Now, Pauline,' he started.

'My name is Paulie, if you want to use it. And I'll call you John.'

'Well, I don't think...'

'I tell you what. You don't call me Paulie, and I won't call you John.' She sat back in her seat.

'Would you like a cigarette?' he said, pushing across the table an unopened packet with a lighter on top. She pushed it back. 'I don't smoke. And I don't trade cigs or drugs. You've been watching too many TV movies. And you haven't read my file.'

He looked round. 'Can I get you a cup of coffee?'

'I don't mind that.'

Five minutes later he returned to the bare little room,

balancing two cartons of coffee in his hand. 'I thought I'd join you. Can we start again?' He smiled a faintly nervous smile but his eyes were steady. 'I'll call you Paulie, if I may, and you can call me John.'

They drank in silence for a few seconds. He tapped her weighty file, on the table in front of him. 'Bit of a hard life, then, Paulie.'

'I wonder if *your* file's that thick,' she said. 'They'll have one on you, you know.'

'Can you tell me about it?'

'About what?'

'About your life. Anything.'

'Anything? Like once I was high on magic mushrooms and went through the whole process of my own birth all over again?'

'Really?' He leaned back in his chair, his face neutral. 'I've heard this can happen.'

She drank the bitter coffee. 'Have you heard the one about being in the middle of all the streaming light, the brilliant silver surging forward, where someone heard their mother scream, their mother dying? Then their father sobbing?'

'No. No. I haven't heard that one.' There was a long pause. He fiddled with his pencils. 'So your dad brought you up?

'Well, I was in care a short while, I think. After she died. When I was a baby. Then he brought me home and we clung together to survive the tide of life.'

He opened the file. 'I've read some of your depositions. You have a way with words, Paulie.'

'I suppose I should say thank you.'

'This is hard, Paulie. I have to be direct. There's so

little time. Can you tell me, in your own words, about your father?'

'My father was an angel. He worked and he worked with a great leaden weight on his back, the fact that he had lost her. They were twin souls. There was no night when I didn't hear him crying. But he tried with me. He really did. Read me stories. Taught me my numbers. Took me to the pictures. We saw *Grease* together four times. He bought me an encyclopedia. That was when he was working. I could name every capital city in the world before I was eight. We had take-aways and fish and chips and lots of eggs and beans. I often think prison food's very similar.'

'So you coped together?'

'Well, yes. Just about. Some people didn't approve, though. He used to keep me up way past my bedtime and talk about the history of the world. The War. The Cold War. The Nuclear Threat. He was up on all of that. But always, even when I was very little, I knew he had this leaden weight on his back. Because *she* wasn't there. That he'd lost *her* for ever, like he'd lost a leg and an arm. Or half his body. He was crippled. Crippled for life. It was like he was shell-shocked, like those guys in the First World War. Did you see that film *Regeneration*? All about that, that was. A neat film.'

'It must have been very hard on a child, hard on you.'

She shrugged. 'It was hard on him. I understood that.'

'But it was hard on you. So small.'

She stared at him, and then pushed her hand through her hair, making it even more spiky. 'You don't understand.'

They sat on in silence. She turned her plastic cup round and round.

'So, you were coping?' He tried again,

'We were all right. That was, until he was made redundant. The usual sob story. After thirty years etc. etc. Thought he was indispensable, he did.'

'And that was it?'

'That was it. He started to drink seriously then, and stopped going out. Sent me out for the booze and the cigarettes. The weekly groceries. He wouldn't go across the door. I've read about it since. *Agoraphobia*. We still talked quite a bit. He was still kind ... kind of ... interested in what I was up to. At school and that.'

'Did no-one try to help?'

She laughed. 'Where have you been? This was the Eighties. *No such thing as society*. Remember? He didn't want me to say anything. Didn't want me to tell. He said they'd take me back into care. He said he needed me with him. That it was me kept him alive.'

'The redundancy money wouldn't last forever, I suppose.'

'It didn't. He'd paid off the house. There was a little pension that paid the electric and gas. Then nothing.'

'What did you do then? What about unemployment benefit?'

'He wouldn't go out. Remember? Wouldn't go out of the house. Not for that or anything.'

'So what did you do?'

She stood up and went to look out of the window. Two girls were trundling a dinner trolley along the path shepherded by a prison officer who whistled as he walked along. 'Well, first I sold the encyclopedia ... anyway, you know what I did. It's in that file you've got there. You don't need to ask.'

'You need to tell me. I need you to tell me, Paulie.'

'I robbed the stuff. Food. Clothes. Sold some of that, and we got along.'

'And you got him his booze?'

'Yeah. He couldn't manage without it.'

'But one day you got sick of all this.'

'That's right.'

'So you…'

'Ran away. Just one night. I ran away to the coast. It was bloody freezing under that pier.'

'And when you got back…'

She turned round and leaned against the window. She was a shadow against the bars. He couldn't see her face. 'And when I got back he was dead and if you want me to tell you about that you can go fuck yourself.'

'Yes. Right.' He shuffled the paper and flicked through the file. 'You'd better come and sit down again, Paulie. If an officer comes in and finds you out of the seat he'll whip you away and our interview will have to come to an end.' He needed to see her face.

She sat down again. 'I've read about it, since, you know. In one of the Sunday Magazines. *Spontaneous combustion*, it's called. It comes somehow from inside you. You burn slowly and nothing around you burns. It's science, though, not magic.'

He looked at her sharply. Her voice had lost its laconic drawl. It had an edge.

She went on. 'I read about it. Saw a programme about it on TV.'

He shook his head. 'It's a myth, Paulie. Not science.'

179

'Well that's what happened. I must have had at least a dozen people talking to me, in that year after he died. Trying to make me say I'd done it. And I hadn't. So I wouldn't say it, just to make them happy. They'd have been happy if I'd said that I did do that, burn my dad alive.'

He flicked to a different part of the file. Then he took a cigarette himself, and lit it. It was a long time since he'd had a smoke. 'Tell me about Charlie.'

She smiled faintly. 'He had golden hair and a lot of charm,' she said. 'And he was a bad boy. … And he was a robber, a drug addict and a sponger.'

'Did he sponge on you, then?' John Kebler said, too quickly.

She shrugged. 'It might have looked like that.'

'But you were a teacher … and he was a … a ne'er-do-well.'

She smiled openly. 'Ne'er-do-well. Now that's an old fashioned word, John Kebler! I wouldn't'a thought you were that old.'

His eyes narrowed. She noticed his long lashes as he lowered his gaze. 'I need to remind you, Paulie Smith, that your freedom's on the table here. Understanding what happened…'

She sighed. 'OK. OK … Charlie was a ne-er-do-well. He robbed, he scrounged, and he dug stuff. But he had golden curls and a great charm. Queenie used to say he must have looked like Lord Byron. The bad Lord Byron. Mad, bad and dangerous to know.'

He let that go. 'Then you lost your job.'

'Well Bernie, Charlie's uncle, lost me my job. Poison pen letter to the school about us living in a squat. He was a wanker of the first order.'

'Why d'he do that?'

''Cause he tried it on with me,' she said calmly. 'And I kneed him in the groin.'

'So he told them…'

'I was a nasty person, implied I was a junkie or worse. They were so sniffy at the school that I just walked out.'

John Kleber flicked his ash into his empty coffee cup and waited.

'And, of course, it's that uncle, that poison penner, baying for my blood now. He said I swore I'd kill Charlie because of another girl.'

'Is it true?'

She smiled. 'The only other girl in Charlie's life was the White Princess.'

'Cocaine?'

'You've got it. Brown, we call it.'

'What did you do when you lost your job?'

'Well. He'd had a close shave with the cops, so he couldn't go out. He was lying low.'

'So?'

'I went out. Grafting. Shoplifting. I was used to that because I'd done it before, when I was caring for my Dad.'

He peered at the file. 'Very successfully, I believe.'

She shrugged. 'It was a living. It bought the food and the booze. It got Charlie his fixes. You're looking for me to say this but in some ways it was like being back with my father.'

'Did you never use the stuff yourself?'

'If you look hard enough in the file you'll see. I did … a few Es … up until … up until that thing happened to my Dad. But not since. Never since.'

181

'Why do you think that is? '

She shrugged. 'I've read it somewhere. I'm not an addictive personality. Funny, that, isn't it? Not even booze. Charlie was the opposite, he was on everything. Except sex.'

John Kebler looked at her. 'Did you resent that? No sex? Why was that?'

'Resent?' She shook her head. 'My golden boy! Stoned half the time, couldn't rouse himself for sex in the end, even when he was comparatively fresh. The drugs do that to them. But you know that, don't you?'

He looked at her carefully. 'You're very, very bright, d'you know that?'

'Are you trying to be patronising?' Then she nodded. 'I've always known it, but it's been bugger all use to me so far. Just see that file.' She looked at her watch. She felt very tired.

'Bear with me, Paulie. I know it's hard, but I want you to tell me what you think happened to Charlie.'

She sighed again. 'Well, that day I'd been out on the graft, then I went to the pub where he's usually waiting for me and the stuff I'd grafted - six pairs of Donna Karen jeans that day. I was pleased with myself. But Charlie wasn't there. I gave them to the old bag that sells them on and I get back to the squat just in time to see the fire engines putting the fire out. A lot of our stuff was soaking, thrown onto the pavement. Curtains, Charlie's brass kettles. But all my books ... were burnt. I had two hundred and seventeen books. I used to spend half my pay on books.' She turned the plastic cup round and round on the Formica top of the table. 'The fence, the old bag at the pub, denied ever seeing me, so that put me in the soup, time-wise.'

'And Charlie was burnt to ... he died.'

'Yes. Charlie died.' She pursed her lips.

'Can you tell me, Paulie, what you think happened?'

'It'll be in there,' she nodded at the bulky file. 'They say I set it alight, that I burnt Charlie. Don't they?'

'You tell me what you think happened.'

She took another very deep breath. 'I'd caught him at it before. He loved chips, did Charlie. He got me to get corn oil from the shop. Said he was gonna fry sausages and have some chips. On the fire d'you see? We could only use the fire. No power. Well, there was another time when I came back and he'd been frying chips on the fire and had gone to sleep on the couch. When I came back the place was full of smoke. The fire had not caught in the room, though. Not that first time. I came back in time that first time.'

'So you think this time that's what happened? The room did catch fire?'

She nodded.

'And do you feel guilty, Paulie, about that? About ... leaving Charlie to do that. To burn himself to death?'

She stared at him. 'Why should I feel guilty? I feel sad. I couldn't be more sad. He was a scamp, Charlie, but he had golden curls, and, like I said, he had a great deal of charm. I loved him.' She looked at her watch. 'Look, can I go? I've finished now. Nothing more to tell you.'

He closed the file and stood up. 'Thank you Paulie Smith. You've been very helpful.' She was at the door. She turned to smile at him. 'Have I? But who have I been helping, John Kebler. You or me?

28 SURVIVING ON THE IN

'… It is, dark but not pitch dark.   Adrenaline is running through my brain like larks. I'm awake but not woken by a dream. This is some thing outside. Outside of me. Luminous pearl light. I stretch my eyes wide.' The magnet that is my body pulls light through the crack between the salt-green curtains.

The dark dissolves, I can make this thing out now. Above me. Hanging above me. Hanging, not floating: a tangle of black rope or thick wool. It doesn't quite have the form of a spider's web but still it contains the same delicate whispering menace.

I slip out of my body and swim across to the door, looking in vain for the handle. Of course. There wouldn't be a handle. I raise my hand to batter the panelled wood but my hand makes no more sound than if I were beating pizza dough, or bubble wrap. I hold my hands up against the light and, peering closely, see that my fingers are bleeding and my nails are broken.

I slip away back into my body and now I watch the girl at the door. I watch her and think what a pity it is. My fingers are neat. Always neat. Filed oval with white tops, in the French style for that natural look. There is no reason to spoil them. Surely? '

From *Behind the Door* by Paulie Smith

Lilah was out from under the blanket and coping well,

taking classes on the Wing, with Queenie and the others. And now she had signed in for computer studies. Getting the hang of that, too. She had a regular pad mate now, a lugubrious girl they called Slim, because she was so fat. But during Association Lilah would look out for Christine and Paulie and the others from the van. She would slide onto a bench beside them and mostly kept quiet. Despite being quiet she was popular among the women. The women cherished any thing of beauty. Good looks in here were sought after. Starved of the beauty and colour of magazines, the glamour of models and singers, they would scout substitutes among themselves on the inside, and slake their thirst by looming around, being alongside, those women whose looks and style were near the ideal.

Lilah's hair was much admired. It was not easy to take care of your hair on the inside. There was little choice of shampoo and less of conditioner but Lilah made the best of it. Out of the tight plaits now, newly conditioned and washed, it dropped like corded sunshine into the small of her back.

In those days in prison the cutting of women's hair could only happen in the workshop under supervision. Christine told the others of a prison she'd once been where a proper hairdresser came to visit, but the others found that hard to believe.

The occasional hairdressing session was seen as a treat: the chance to get your hair out of your eyes; to put your appearance into some semblance of order and normality. You would dream, sometimes, of seeing your hair rise like silk from the airy nudge of the blow-dryer: of looking through the salon mirror and meeting the confident, professional gaze of the hairdresser, no older then yourself, as she teases your hair through her long fingers.

Not here, though. Not now. Radio One blares and pings off the steel sewing machines. The women duck their heads over the machines, sewing bibs which the women slip on at visiting time to label them insider. Or they sew overalls for the men in one of the men's prisons.

A girl called Alison Redgrove, in for dealing, was doing the cutting today, watched closely by the officers. Later in the day she'll get her pay from the women in tobacco or Crunchie bars. Alison was a tall, thin girl who liked to get a laugh out of anything, at any cost. She'd served her time, years ago, as a hairdresser. Never worked properly, though, on the out. Too stoned to get up in the morning, and as well as that she stole the perm lotions to sell and buy gear.

But she could do the business with hair, could Alison. Locks of hair fell to the dusty workroom floor: blonde curls, black curls like coiled liquorice, long strands of hair, striped ginger and cream. Lilah, who took the last turn, was pleased to be getting her hair cut. It had lost its blunt-cut edge months ago and her fringe was in her eyes.

As Alison set about her task with Lilah the other girls glanced across from their machines. Some stopped working, their wide eyed gazes fixed, watching Alison as she made a horrific knife-and-fork job of Lilah's hair. She made such a jagged, moth-eaten-carpet job of it that, one by one, all the girls stopped machining and watched open-mouthed.

('No mirrors. See?' explained an outraged Paulie to Queenie later that day. 'It's a workshop for sewing overalls for TWOCCers and burglars in the men's place.

No-one ever said it was a salon! No mirrors, see?')

Lilah stood up, shook her hair out, and asked the women what they thought. 'Nice!' 'It's all right!' 'Well, funky…'

Christine and Paulie, on the corridor, told Lilah the truth. Lilah saw for herself in the milky mirror in the cell. That night she spent half the night in her cell brushing her hair. The other half of the night she spent crying. Slim told her to pack it in. There were worse things to worry about than hair, she said.

The next day Christine stopped Alison Redgrove on her way to the workshop. 'Why d'you do that, Alison? Why the hell d'you spoil the lass's hair? You're much better than that with hair.'

'For a laugh. Cos she's too fucking gorgeous, that's why,' said Alison sulkily. Alison's two friends were suddenly at her shoulder. An officer, sharp to the sense of trouble, elbowed his way past the women in the narrow corridor and made his way towards the source of the yelling.

'Spoiled! You spoiled her fucking hair.' Christine screamed and pushed Alison against the wall. All out fight! The women crowded round and cheered. Queenie felt her way backwards until she was right at the back of the crowd, babbling in vain to the Great Ones to come to stop this, stop this!

Alison lashed out with her fist and Christine smacked her in the face. Alison's friend jumped on Christine and Maritza grabbed one of her arms and tried to pull her back. Alison turned and winged Maritza in the eye. Paulie got hold of Alison who turned and hit her across the cheek with her closed fist. The officer yanked Christine off the pile and Christine turned swiftly and butted him in the face with her broad forehead. As he curled up on the floor, hands on his bloody face Christine leaned down and unclipped his keys from his belt. She held the keys above her head and the women cheered.

'No, Christine, no!' Lilah made her way through the crowd and wrenched the keys from Christine's's hands. Queenie covered her ears as the air was suddenly pieced through with shrill alarms, threaded through with the sound of feet padding across the tarmac as dozens of officers ran full pelt towards the wing where the alarm had been raised.

That was it. In minutes all the women in the ruck were pinioned by officers. The rest of the women were marshalled back to their cells.

Queenie looked fearfully back towards Paulie, held now against the wall by two female officers. Then she trailed back to the cell on her own. She sat on her bunk with her hands over her face, rocking backwards and forwards, more truly miserable than she'd been for many years.

It was an hour before Paulie got back to the cell. She had a great bruise down the side of her face. She flung herself into the chair. Queenie looked up at her and said timidly. 'That was a bad business, dear. Poor little Lilah. Poor Maritza. Poor you.'

'And you should see Maritza's black eye!' Paulie laughed bitterly. 'Bad? We're all out of here tomorrow, Queenie. Out of it. Scattered like chaff before the wind. Prisons all over the country.'

'Out of it?'

'Split up. Me, Christine and Lilah, shipped out of this place. Even little Maritza who was only trying to help.

And that bloody Alison and her mate.   Troublemakers, see? I think the tin lid was when Christine lifted the keys. And when she bashed the officer.'

'But you didn't do that, my dear. You went to help your friends.'

'Tarred with the same brush.   That's what the Governor said.'

'But I'll be left here on my own!' Queenie wailed.

'That's what it looks like, Queenie.' Paulie sighed and knelt beside Queenie where she sat hunched up on her bunk. 'Don't let it get to you, love. Just keep your head down till you get out. That's all you need to do. And I'll say your poems and think of you.'

Later, the prison night closed round them as they lay wide awake in their cell; together for the last time.   The noise in the yard tonight was greater than ever, as the communal voice roared its commentary on the dramatic events of the day. When that had all faded into the prison twilight, Queenie chanted, line by line, verse by verse, chanted every fine poem she knew at the top of her voice. She did it to comfort Paulie, who was lying wide-awake in the bunk above her. An officer banged on the door and told her to stop the caterwauling.   But still she kept on, line after line, verse after verse.

29 I DO KNOW MARITZA MOLLOY

Paulie: 'Twenty-nine. Thirty.' The doors, maroon and midnight blue, shine like snail trails in the afternoon light. The white plastic window frames cut sharp lines against the red brick. The front lawns are communal, kept trim by the council, I'd guess. A show estate, I suppose. I've seen much worse.

'Thirty three.' This house is neat and trim like all the rest. Maritza opens the door. Her hair is pulled up on top and fastened with a scrunchie. Her face, clear of make up, still looks very young, even though she must be over forty now. She pulls me inside. 'Paulie! . The woman told me on the phone ... I read about you in the papers. Come on in.'

The little sitting room is immaculate. On the table by the window stand tulips in a plain glass vase, the green stems refracting just a bit as they hit the water. On the mantelpiece is a tall vase with three lilies. The scent reminds me of Charlie on that first day.

'Sit down, Paulie.' She has a tray ready - black tin painted with red roses; a white plate with two types of biscuit laid out alternately to make a pattern. 'You look all right, Paulie, considering. I read about it in the paper like I said. Lots of those old photos. Of that time when you went into prison. You looked a bit different then, mind you.'

'My punk days? Queenie thought I was a boy, you know. That day in the van.'

'Queenie!' She shakes her head. 'Look. I'll just scald the coffee and we can settle down.'

Now I'm feeling very uneasy. I might be Maritza's distant cousin or slight acquaintance. I look around the room. What do I want in a place like this? This place has nothing to do with me. Not a thing. Who is she, this Maritza Molloy? Why do I think I know her? I should think of something cute to say, so I can get away quickly. Make my getaway.

She's back, smart cafetière in hand. 'Now!' She sits down and leans across to pour the coffee, and then she looks up at me. 'The first days on the out are awful, aren't they? Always looking behind you for permission to spit. Calling the shop lady miss and the bus conductor sir?'

I relax, breathe out very slowly, then lean forward to pick up my white china mug. I do know Maritza Molloy. 'What about being able to lie full length in a bath?' I say. 'I had three baths on the first day I got out Ritzy. Three! With bubbles.

'And going to the shop to buy your own food. Three- colour salads! A piece of steak!'

'And the roads! How long the roads are and the cars are so fast.'

'And the clothes on people in the street, colours so bright they dazzle you!'

'And using a steel knife and fork! And scissors! I cut my own hair with scissors the first day I got out,' I say swinging my long bob to demonstrate.

A shadow like a curtain falls across her childlike face. 'Yeah. What about the time that girl cut Lilah's hair. Awful.'

'Yeah.'

We are silent for a minute, then she says, 'Of course I could only say these things to you. Or one of the others.' She pauses and flicks her head to encompass the world. 'They expect you to be jumping with joy when you get out.'

'You stagger around, buffeted from sight to sight. Seasick, with all this bright stuff shafting in on you.'

We are silent again. Then I take another breath. 'You're looking good yourself, Maritza. Not quite the Miss Prim you were when you first came inside.'

'Christine, you remember Christine? She once asked me was I the mother my boys knew when I was the mother my boys knew? Wise one, that girl. Tragic. She changed me.'

'Have you seen her around?'

Maritza shakes her head. 'Not since then. Didn't seem worth it, chasing after all that. Going backwards somehow.'

So, what am I doing here, chasing all that? 'How long did you do, in the end, Maritza?'

'Could have been more. I got four years, served two.' she says. 'Judge was lenient because they got all the money back, and I pleaded guilty. And I got a good psychiatrist's report in the end. Stress from the divorce and all that. Deprived childhood.'

'Deprived childhood? You?'

'The psych seemed to think so. Fellow called John Kebler. Didn't you know him? Wasn't he the one who was interviewed on the radio about you? He was very helpful to me. I only hacked two and a bit years in the end.'

'He's a good enough sort. He really helped me with the appeal you know. I'm staying in his house,' I say. 'Just for the present.'

'Good,' she says. 'That's something.'

'It's just for the present.'

She glances round. 'I'd offer you a bed myself but…'

'No. No. No need at all. So what about those sons of yours? Are they around?'

She shakes her head. 'Not Rory. Rory never came back from Canterbury. I never see him. He's in London now. Doing a law degree, funnily enough.'

'Pity you don't see him,' I say. 'You could have given him the inside track on all that shit.' For some reason we both splutter with laughter at that.

'So … Sam?'

Her face lightens. 'Sam? He came to me soon as he could. He ran away from them, from Roland and his computer woman in Canterbury. He ran away to me. They'd had a bit of a hard time with him and were only too delighted to hand him over, poor things.'

'That's good, then. You've got Sam with you.'

She shakes her head. 'It is, and it isn't. His exams were shot, with all that running away and he had to retake his year. But he still only scraped them. All messed up really. All my fault, of course. Desmond blames me.'

'He would, wouldn't he? Is Sam working?'

She shakes her head again. 'Work experience. He's learned how to paint and how to plaster, but no real work.' She glances round the trim sitting room. 'He keeps this place up to scratch, though. And he does painting for people around the place. If the dole catches up with him he'll be in trouble. Then, of course, there's Amy.'

My head comes up, 'What?'

She smiles widely and collects a picture from the sideboard and passes it to me. Big round eyes. Curls dropping over her ears. 'She's three-and-a-half.'

'Who's this?' I say stupidly. 'Who's Amy?'

'She's mine.' Maritza takes the picture from me and holds it up to the light. 'I met this man the day I came out. In a café. Retired greengrocer. He kind of took me under his wing. No funny business. Mind you. He kind of took care of me. Reminded me of my father. Then he took me out for a meal one time. I felt so sorry for him and we had such a dizzy time that we ended up in bed. That was the end of it, of course. A kind of incest when you think of it. We were both too embarrassed to meet after that. Then a few months later I'm pregnant and horrified.'

'Didn't you…?'

'An abortion? No. It didn't occur to me. I don't know why.' She sips the last of her coffee. 'Anyway along comes Amy and I can't thank the greengrocer enough. He left me with this great gift. And he sends useful money now and then. Now Sam and Amy and me, we are our own kind of family. Those two are dotty about each other.'

On cue, there is a rattle at the door and young voices in the hallway. I get to my feet, ready for flight. 'No. No. Sit down,' she says. 'Sit down. Stay with us.'

They bustle in, the child first, then a tall, handsome boy with blond curls. My heart leaps and then steadies. Charlie. No. Not Charlie. Sam. This boy's name is Sam. He is not much younger than Charlie was when I first met him. The child at his knees is a scrap of a thing with the same blonde hair. She has blue eyes, though, and she wears round owl-like child's glasses.

Maritza put an arm out towards them. 'Here is Sam, and here is Amy. This is Paulie Smith, Sam. You know about Paulie.'

His hand, when he shakes mine, is thin and strong. 'I read about you in the papers,' he says. 'Bloody shame that...'

'I'm Amy,' said the little one, putting her own hand out. I shake the hand which is plump and firm as a marrow. Now I have to go. This is too much. I want to cry. 'I have to go, Maritza.'

'Don't go. Stay for tea.'

'No. No,' I lie. 'I have to be somewhere. Promised someone.' I scrabble clumsily in my bag and pull out one of the slim volumes. 'I brought this for you.'

She looks at the volume, then hands it to Sam, who leafs through with interest. 'It's... Well... The poems are from those first weeks at Bronte House. I didn't write them then. I wrote them much later, in another prison. But it's all about those first weeks.' I'm embarrassed now. It seems like so much showing off. Who the hell do I think I am?

Sam whistles and sniffs the cover of the book. 'Cool,' he says.

'Can I see the book?' says Amy.

'I tell you what, Amy. Marmite sandwiches!' says Sam. 'How about Marmite sandwiches?' He swings her up on his shoulders and they go through to the kitchen.

Maritza strokes the back of the book with her hand. 'Thank you, Paulie.' She flicks the book open and sees her name. 'Thank you for thinking of me.'

WENDY ROBERTSON

'Yes,' I say abruptly. 'Yes. What about Christine? Do you know where Christine is? Or Queenie?'

She shakes her head. 'I suppose you just want to leave it behind. Forget it all.' She meets my gaze. 'I even thought twice before I told that woman you could have my address.'

'Good that you did.' I'm in a hurry now, to get out. I know I won't come again.

Her hand is on the door handle when she stops. 'Lilah! I do know where you can find Lilah.'

'You've got her address?'

She shakes her head. 'No. But I saw her at the clinic where I go with Amy sometimes. For jabs and things. She usually has two children round her skirts. I was right at the other side of the waiting room, but when I struggled through the crowd to get to her she was gone. Mrs. Caperling! They called her. Mrs. Caperling. And she must live on this estate. The clinic only serves this estate.' She reaches up and gives me a peck on the cheek. 'Keep in touch, Paulie, keep in touch.'

I mumble something, but know - even as I say it - that I won't come back here. At the corner of the street I turn and look back and there they are, waving. Sam with Amy clinging to him like a monkey, and Maritza beside him. Happy. Settled together in their own little family.

On the bus, trundling back into town, I start to think about Lilah. The telephone book. I would look up Lilah in the telephone book.

Caperling!

30 NEW BOOKS

I've had to tell Fiona Kebler what I am trying to do here. After all, it's her telephone on which I'm going to make calls to the twenty-nine Caperlings. It might be less, of course. But Lilah might be the last in the list of Caperlings.

'Oh, yes,' Fiona fluttered her hand at me. 'Just do it, Paulie.'

'I'll pay, for the calls. Make a note and pay.'

She looks at me for a second, then says, 'Well. If that's what you want, Paulie.' She sets me up at the desk in John Kebler's consulting room. Compared with the clutter of the rest of the house, this room is pristine. Polished furniture. Pale green carpet. Neat modern desk, completely bare except for a grey-blue lump of crystal. Computer console to one side. Books standing up like soldiers in two massive bookcases. The telephone has its own small trolley to the other side. He must really need to keep the desk clear. Under the window are two very deep chairs. No psychiatrist's couch - now that's a surprise.

'Pull the phone by the desk, Paulie. That's what John does.' Fiona moves the phone for me then puts the baby, who I now know is a girl called Keeva, onto the other hip and leaves me to it.

I sit in John Kebler's chair and put my notebook beside the phone. I am too conscious that he has sat in this chair himself. Has breathed this air. It's the phoniest, the corniest, most stupid thing that I'd get – well - feelings

197

for John Kebler. Like Maritza and her greengrocer. Like some savage fairy tale. The first man you set eyes on, you're hooked. You're a sucker for company, for confirmation of that part of you that is seductive and free. This life mirror for people like Maritza and me can only be male.

I've seen John Kebler twice since I moved into this house but that's quite enough. Once was when I went to join them for drinks in their cluttered sitting room where the free-flowing conversation was mostly between the two of them. The spotlight was off me, which was very comforting. The other time was when he came down to the basement to bring me the boxes of books that I'd sent here from the prison.

I opened the first box while he was there and shut it quickly, my flesh chilling at the unmistakable prison smell which was released into the warm air of my little room. 'I can't,' I said. 'They smell of prison. Dust. Isolation. Pain. Women.'

He looked carefully at me, then said, 'Would you like me to unpack them? No? Shall I take them back upstairs? Yes, I'll do that and bring them to you when you're ready.' Then he was gone and I wished like mad that he'd stayed.

I'm getting some very stroppy answers on the phone, three of which tell me to fuck off and sell my stuff elsewhere. I have a hit on the fourteenth call. A man answers. 'Could I speak to Lilah?' I say. 'I am a friend of hers from school.'

'Lilah's not in, sorry.' The voice is not young.

'Could I leave a message?'

'Hang on a bit while I get a bit of paper.'

There are mutterings in the background. Children's

voices. The shriek and blare of a television game show. 'Now then, pet. A message, yer say?'

'Just that Paulie rang.'

'Pauline, yer say?'

'No. Paulie. P-A-U-L-I-E.'

'Aye. Got that.'

'And can you ask her to ring me on this number?'

We have three tries to get the number right. I'm shaking when I put down the phone. Lilah is not a common name but Lilah Caperling might not know me from Adam. Or, better, she might not know me from Eve.

So I start telephoning again, working my way down the rest of the list. Every last one. Three more outright insults, the rest just sorry that there was no Lilah there. I put the telephone neatly back onto its table and rub the desk clean of my fingerprints with the sleeve of my sweatshirt. I walk around the room, poking at the books, picking up the crystals. Then, reluctantly, I leave.

Fiona has coffee brewing in the kitchen and insists I join her. 'Come on, Paulie. Keeva's in her cot. I have a rare ten minute's breather.'

I so want to dislike her. I want to think she's a messy scruffy snob with a cut glass accent. But I can't and she isn't. I don't know what to say. I take refuge in talking about the house. 'So, how long have you lived here?' How inane that sounds. Stupid.

She glances around the kitchen. 'Here? Well, I've lived here for four years. John? He's lived here probably twenty or so.'

I have many questions and I can't ask one. But, even so, she answers them.

'How did I meet him? I was his student. Before he was full time at the university he taught odd vocational courses.' She catches my look and answers another unasked question. 'No, I didn't steal him from his wife. He'd been a widower five or six years by then.'

'So you're a psychiatrist too?'

She laughed. 'Heavens no. The course he taught was some quirky thing called "Pathology as Literary Explanation". Crap, actually. Half-formed notions in peculiar-speak. I told him so and we got on like a house afire.'

'So that was a literature course? You did literature?'

'No, actually. It was a general old BA. Scraped a third, then married John. He and Keeva are my career at present. I'll probably do something eventually.'

I sit here, so consumed with envy that I can taste it. I resent the airy certainties, the patent happiness, the purposeful contentment, the confidence that would allow her to supervise a house which was like a slum, as though presiding over a palace.

(My father is in front of the fire, slumped in his chair, his eye, half apologetic, half hopeful. Around him is our house, kept desperately clean by me. Every surface rubbed, every crumb cleared away. The fireplace swept and polished with Mr Kleen.)

'So, Paulie,' she says. 'How…'

But now I'm barging out of the room, falling over a child's Teddy Bear and a funny plastic bike. I scramble to my feet and walk out quickly. No backward glance to show her the tears on my face. My pathetic self-pity. I'm living in a state of pathetic chaos, or chaotic pathos, can't quite say which. I throw myself on my bed and pull the blanket up over my head as I did, so many times, in the last six years in my cell. I can't do this thing, being on the out. I can't do this thing. I can't do this. I can't do this. I can't do this.

The room is dark when I emerge from under the blanket. I put on the lights and take a long shower, standing under the faltering spray for twenty minutes, until my flesh is cold, despite the pulsing hot water. I step outside. Put on the wrap which I brought away from the hotel. (I must take it back. What possessed me?) I put on the kettle, wash the cups and find that the water won't run away from the sink. In despair I open the little cupboard under the sink and peer inside. 'Fuck fuck fuck fuck fuck!'

A voice behind me says, 'Can I help?'

I scrabble backwards to see John Kebler's polished brown shoes, his creased cotton pants. Shit.

'I'm sorry. I knocked,' he said. 'Fiona was worried. She said you were upset.'

He helps me to my feet and I'm too conscious of his hand on my arm. I pull the wrap closely round my body. 'I'm OK. Tell Fiona I'm sorry. Nothing to do with her. Panic attack, something like that.'

'You're all right now?'

I sit down in a chair, my knees very close together. 'Like I said. Big panic over nothing.'

'It'll happen from time to time. Look, there are counsellors, resettlement people. I can put you in touch…'

'I've got all those fucking numbers. They gave me them at the prison. I'll do it myself.'

He is standing by the window. I wish he would sit down. But I can't ask him to do that. Too friendly.

'Fiona says you have a number for Lilah? Will you see her? What if she doesn't call?'

'I have an address too. From the telephone book. I'll call round.'

'Might be risky.'

'Still, I'll do it.'

He is staring at me.

'What is it?' I say.

He blinks and almost shakes his head as though dislodging a fly. 'I have something for you.'

He goes back to the door and carts in three purple carrier bags. 'Here,' he says. Onto my bed, he tips out a pile of brand new books. The deliciously pregnant smell of new paper pervades the air. Then he puts the books in line and their gleaming covers shine up at me in the light of the bedroom lamp. Sylvia Plath. William Carlos Williams. Yeats. Two Brontës. Ted Hughes. Seamus Heaney. Raymond Carver. Margaret Atwood. Angela Carter. Sara Paretsky. Joseph Brodskey. Three dictionaries. Two Thesaurae. And yet more. These are the newly published duplicates of the books in the prison boxes that I couldn't bear to touch.

'I tried to match what you had. The shop sourced them for me.' He actually sounds anxious. 'I hope it is OK?'

I pick up the books and put them to my face, one after the other, smell their pristine smell, turn the pages and the dense print and the gleaming white spaces dance before my eyes. I want to lick them.

'I thought you should have them,' he says gruffly. 'They're your badges of survival. They're a kind of reflection of you – for you. Part of what makes you

202

special.'

'They're all special,' I say. 'They are a reflection of me - Christine and Queenie and the others.'

'I know that.'

Then I really do cry, and I am in his arms and he is rocking me to and fro, crooning over the top of my wet hair like a mother over her baby. 'Shh. Shh,' he says. 'Shh.' I can feel his heart beating against my cheek. My legs are lined up along his. And then we leap apart and there are feet – yards - miles between us.

I pick up the books, and pile them in my arms, creating a properly concrete barrier between him and me. 'Thank you John Kebler. Thank you.'

He looks me in the eye. 'I can't do enough for you,' he says soberly, staring me in the eyes. 'I can't do enough.' Then he's gone and I make my mind blank by organising the books in alphabetical order on the little shelf by the bed.

31 AT THE RUNNING MAN

The next morning Fiona comes downstairs to tell me that Lilah has phoned, left the number again and asked me to telephone her at ten o'clock.

'Paulie! Paulie Smith? I can't believe it.' The voice is bright enough. She's certainly not still under the blanket. 'I read about you in the papers. I told this lot here that we knew each other. That I knew you.'

I am smiling. 'Yeah. The thing is, Lilah, I've got something for you. Can we meet?'

'Well. Yes. We could.' She is clearly not too sure.

'Only for a few minutes.'

'There's such a houseful here. Tumbling over each other. You never get a minute.'

'What about a pub? A café near you?' I will not let her go.

'One on the coast road, called The Running Man…'

'Today?'

'OK then. One o'clock.'

Sitting in the corner seat in The Running Man, Lilah's easy to recognise. She's still quite a beauty. Long, flat hair. Of course. I remember the tale of her mother ironing her hair. I wonder who irons it now? She stands up. We face each other awkwardly.

She fishes in her bag. 'I'll get you something.'

I have to let her. 'Coke with ice,' I say.

'Not beer? Wine?'

'I don't drink,' I say. 'I never drink.'

'Oh yes. I remember. While we were planning that first kick into a bottle, you were saying how pure you were.'

Lilah seems easier, more relaxed, when she comes back with the drinks. She looks me over.

'Don't tell me I've changed,' I say.

She shrugs. 'We've all changed in six years, Paulie.'

'So how about you? How have you changed?'

She laughs. 'Well, apart from the wine, I'm not on anything, if that's what you mean.'

We sit in silence for a second. Then I try, 'Getting through that gate's a queer feeling, isn't it?'

'Yeah. I was dizzy for a week when I got out. Falling-down dizzy.'

'How was it? You were beginning to kick the stuff in those fist weeks.'

'Yeah. You could say that. Seventeen months was long enough to be right off it, like. But I did go back with Jonno when I got out. And he was still dealing and using. He really didn't like me not using. So I had to get out of there or I knew I would start. So, back to my mother. My mother was great.' She pauses. 'Jonno OD'd you know.'

I wait.

'I hadn't seen him for months then. I just read it in the paper. D'you know, Paulie, I didn't feel a thing? But I sometimes think ... I know ... if I hadn't had my mother there... I just know I'd have been on the slab beside him.'

There was not much to say. 'So, it's Mrs. Caperling

now then?'

'Yeah. Married. Two kids. A father-in-law who's an old bugger. A job at Asda.'

'Your husband?'

'Dylan? He's OK. Clean as a whistle. Never smoked a fag, never mind grass. Turned on by fishing when the other lads were turned on by skag.' She sounds utterly bored. 'He came to fit my mother's kitchen and it was lust at first sight.'

'Are you happy, Lilah?' Why do I come out with such a fucking, stupid question?

She looked me straight in the eye. 'Me, Paulie? The truth? I haven't been happy since I was eighteen just dancing the night away with my pals on a Friday night.'

There's heartbreak between us, pain. The waste. The waste. I scrabble in my bag and pull out the slim volume. 'I wrote these, Lilah. They're ... well ... about when we were in prison together.' My words are lame and I know the book will mean nothing to her.

She loves the inscription, though. 'Christine! Queenie!' she says. 'All of us! That's cool, Paulie. Really cool.' She might never read a single one of the poems but the book means something to her. I'm glad now that I made all those telephone calls. She tucks the book into her bag.

I can't resist it. 'Will you show it to Dylan?' I say.

Slowly she shakes her head. 'I don't think so Paulie. I think it's very clever and that. But he wouldn't understand. He never wants to know about that time inside. Not even interested when you were in the paper. It's a blank between us.' She pats her bag. 'But, me, I'll treasure it. I promise you.'

I know she will. We have one more drink and she takes my address. 'I'll send you a card at Christmas,' she says. 'We'll keep in touch.' And I know we won't

32 A WALK BY THE OCEAN

The next day I have to telephone my solicitor and Probation to tell them where I am. My solicitor says some broadsheet has been in touch to do a big feature called Injustice, and the Challenge of Life on the Outside. What? I tell him that no way should he tell them my address. No way.

The good news that day is that John Kebler has news of Queenie. Seems she's in some old people's home at Catherstone Bay on the coast. He got this through some persistent canvassing with the Health Services and then Geriatric Care Agency.

A fresh T shirt, a bit of eye-black and I'm ready. John Kebler is hovering in the hall. 'I'll run you, Paulie,' he says. 'I'll take you there.'

'No. I'll go myself. I'm quite capable.'

'Let John take you,' Fiona's voice rings out from the kitchen. 'You'll knock yourself up, darling, racing around like this.'

''Darling!' Shit!

I couldn't make a fuss. Couldn't make a stand. If it had just been him, I'd have definitely insisted on 'No'. But

Fiona - I couldn't say no to her. It would be too vehement, too full of meaning. It would make her wonder. She'd see the truth before he did.

So many firsts! Apart from the taxi coming away from the prison this is the first car I've been in for much more than seven years. Once or twice when I was a student I had a ride in another student's car. Before that, nothing. After that, nothing. This car is comfortable. It glides along. It's the car, mark you, of the older man. Safe. Posh. There's room in the boot for golf clubs, for a carry cot, for a hundred quid's worth of groceries from Sainsbury's.

'Can I ask you something, John Kebler?'

'Anything.' He smells of pinewoods and honey.

'Do you play golf?'

'No. Why? Want a game?'

'No. I just wondered.'

'Why do you call me John Kebler? Not just John?'

I let the car go half a mile. 'To keep the distance,' I say.

'I see.' He pulls up outside Ocean View. 'I'll wait,' he says.

The home is a biggish building just off the strand, within sight of the sea. A small plaque tells me it was once a small hotel serving miners' families for their summer break. There is a ramp outside with attendant wheelchair: symbols of this modern, caring world. A brisk woman presides over reception; an upside down watch moves gently on her broad bosom.

'Queenie?' she says. 'Oh yes. She's in the day room. She does like to see the sea. A bit of a character, is our Queenie.'

As we walk down the corridor I ask, 'Has she been here a long time?'

'I would have to check. I've only been here six months. Here we are.'

The chairs are squared up facing inwards around the room. A rosy faced woman is knitting. Two men are playing draughts. Three women are twittering; it might be an argument or complaint. Only one chair is not placed looking inward on the room. This is planted plumb in the middle of the bay window, back to the room, and face to the sea.

'Here we are Queenie. A visitor for you!' I pull up a chair beside her. Her face is just the same, the pixie-like sharpness etched even deeper. She smiles at me. 'It's not Janine, dear, is it?' Fine creases divide her brow.

I pick up her hand and hold it in mine and she turns hers to grasp my fingers. She pulls herself towards me. Her grasp tightens. 'I know, dear, it's Paulie. My little girl from the prison. How are you, my dear?' Her voice is reedy, missing a note now and then like a worn out violin, but it still has a teacher's penetration.

'How are you, Queenie?'

'Well it's happening again dear. I fell down some steps and hurt my leg, so I had to go to hospital. Then they parked me here.'

'Is it all right, your leg?'

'The leg? Fine. Gives me a bit of gyp now and then, so I'm still stuck here, dear.'

I look around. 'Doesn't seem too bad.'

She shakes her head. 'They try, poor things, but still it's the same. Shut in and they don't like you to move. It was always like this. They can be so cross when you don't take the pills. Then it's new faces, always new faces. And the undertakers! Nice young men but they're always here in their black anoraks. Fresh faces in black anoraks, their lives before them.' Her voice, needle bright now, penetrates the room. The old people look up, interested. An attendant kneeling down and fastening an old man's slipper with a Velcro tab, cocks her head to listen.

'Shsh, Queenie,' I say. 'Shsh.'

She drops her voice to a whisper. 'It was so much nicer at that place where we were, dear, with you in the top bunk. No silly old people there. Just young ones with bright hair. And they forgot about the pills for quite some time, there, before they remembered.'

The combination of antiseptic lotions, human body smells and dry heat is making me feel sick. 'Would you like to go for a walk Queenie? Perhaps we could go for a walk?'

Her head comes up like a questing bird. 'By the sea? We can walk by the sea?'

It all takes some fixing, but with a flurry of hats, scarves and gloves, and a sprinkle of disapproving stares, we are out of the home. I poke my head into the window of the waiting car. John Kebler is marking some kind of document with fluorescent highlighter. He nods, distracted. 'I'm OK. You go ahead, Paulie.' He glances across at Queenie. 'HI!' he says.

Queenie ignores him and takes my arm. I feel connected. 'The sea,' she says. 'The sea. The Old Man came to me once, striding out of this tide, Paulie. Not long ago. Streaming seaweed. His hair down his back. I was on the sand a good half hour before they came to get me.' She stops and turns to look up at me. 'You have a lot more

211

hair these days, haven't you? Your hair was clipped right over the top then. A boy's crop from an old film. Still, you were nice. A nice little face.'

We walk on.

'I knew you. I know people's faces,' she said. 'Forty years in a classroom. You judge faces. You can tell the good from the bad, the monsters from the angels.'

The seafront is deserted. Suddenly the waves start to swoosh and turn and the wind blows up off the sea and off comes Queenie's hat. She laughs and laughs at this, and pushes me forward. 'Run! Run and get it for me dear!' I chase after it onto a cobbled causeway and down onto the beach.

The hat rolls and rolls this way and that like a squirrel or some other live animal. It takes me a full five minutes to capture it. I turn round and hold it up in my arms like the World Cup. 'We've won! We've won!'

She waves frantically, hanging onto the rail. 'Hooray!' Her reedy voice bounces towards me like a ball in the wind. 'Hooray!'

At the end of the strand is a little café with tin tables and a one-armed bandit in the corner. We order tea and biscuits. She munches hers with appreciation. 'So how are you doing, dear? Where have you been? I've waited a long time for you.'

'You know where I've been. I've been in prison, nearly six years, Queenie.'

She frowns. 'Brontë House?'

'No, other places like Brontë House. Darker places.'

'Six years! My dear girl what did you do to make them lock you away for so long?' Of course none of them knew what I'd done in those weeks at Brontë House: the

212

veil of secrecy, the filament of preservation kept us all taut on the web.

'I didn't do anything, Queenie. Except a bit of shoplifting. But they said then I killed my boyfriend. Burned him to death.'

She stops in her tracks, a hand to her mouth. 'Oh. My dear girl. You didn't do that. Anyone could tell you wouldn't do that. Where was their judgment, those people?'

'They thought from the start I'd done it. Mainly because my father died in a fire eight years before that. They thought I had burned them both.'

'And did you, dear? You didn't! Of course you didn't.'

'No I didn't. And now they're admitting it. Now they've found I told them the truth. Otherwise I'd still have been in prison two, three years more.'

'Dear me. How cruel. And have they said sorry, locking you up like that? That is so bad of them.'

'Oh yes. They're busy saying sorry now. They're giving me a nice present to make me feel better.'

She beams up at me. 'Well, that's all right then!' She puts her arm through mine and we walk along again.

Nearly six years. Six fucking years of dry air and dust. Of eating to order. Working to order. Showering to order. Pissing to order. Six fucking years. But it is all right again. I smile at her. 'It's all right now, Queenie.'

There's this talk, quite a bit of talk, of topping yourself in prison. Women get desperate, down: they feel utterly invisible pushed to one side. But it's not just those who talk of topping themselves who do it. The one time it happened in my experience, the girl was bright and breezy. She'd been a bit down it was true. But she was better.

Bright and breezy, like I say. Then one night, click. Alone in her cell after one changeover. Carefully torn sheets. The care! Think of the care! Then click! The light is out.

There was hell to pay, but what can you do? What could they have done, really?

I never felt like that inside, like, topping myself. Too easy. Too easy for them all. They'd be right, see? But now, meeting and cutting myself adrift again from Maritza, then Lilah, living in an alien cut-glass household with the click and grind of prison keys still echoing in my ears, I don't know. The thought of topping yourself is creeping about there in the back of my mind.

Now, pushing all this away I say chirpily to Queenie, 'Are you happy there, then, at Ocean View?'

She frowns at me. 'Well they try their best, dear. But those old people! So difficult and, to be honest, not much joy. And you see the little girls they get to help! Well. Uncouth, my dear. But they try their best.'

'You don't like it, do you?'

'Well dear, would you? Would you like it? I'm old and I'm batty but I'm still who I am.'

We walk back along the front, arm in arm. The sea is quieter now. The wind has dropped but salt is still in the air. At the home the reception woman is obviously relieved to see us. 'Queenie wanders, you see.' She looks Queenie in the face and raises her voice. 'You wander, don't you, Queenie? You naughty girl.'

Queenie raises her eyes towards me. 'Do you see what I mean, Paulie?'

We settle her down in her window seat and I fish out the small volume. 'Here, Queenie, I brought this for you.'

She puts on her glasses and examines the book very

carefully. She exclaims when she sees her name in the dedication, then reads through two or three of the pieces.

'Oh, my dear girl! Wonderful words. Wise words.'

'I don't really know if they're poetry,' I say defensively. 'They're just bits of writing.'

She pushed the book towards me. 'Read it!' she says. 'Read some of those pieces to me. In your voice.'

I read them out quietly but there are uncomfortable stirrings round the room. The assistant comes over. 'I don't know that we're allowed to do that, readin',' she says, 'in here.'

I close the book and hand it to Queenie.

'They sound wonderful in your voice, dear,' she says. 'I can't think who they remind me of but they are fragile thoughts, but at the same time strong.'

Unlike Maritza and Lilah, Queenie is the one who has taken the book for what it is. She knows the effort I've put into it. For the others it is a very welcome object. A symbol of our shared time. For Queenie it is what it is. 'I'll keep it in my bag, dear, always.' she says. 'It is a treasure.'

'I'll come to see you again.' This time I mean it. I'll not go to see Maritza again, nor Lilah. But I will see Queenie.

'That's nice, dear,' she says. 'It's been lovely to see you. It made me remember our good times.'

John Kebler is still going through papers as I jump back in the car. 'You're bouncing!' he says. 'Good visit?'

'Queenie's just the same. She recognised me. I read my poems to her. She liked them.'

'Wise woman,' he says. The car turns its nose towards the town, purring like the big cat which inspired its design.

We sit in silence for a while. Then, 'I'm gonna get her out,' I say.   'Get her out of that place.'

'Now, Paulie!' John Kebler glances at me, scowling.

'You watch me, John Kebler!' I say.   'You just watch me.'

33 PAULIE'S WEB

I have to make making a conscious effort to clean up my language. I am sick of hearing those awful words drip off my tongue. Inside prison you internalise the potency and satisfaction of four letter words and they pepper your normal language like everyday benedictions.

I remember Maritza once told me a tale about some aunt of hers scouring out her mouth when she was a little girl for saying *damn*! I go to the sink in my little basement room, say *fuck* then fill my mouth with water rub the inside with a bar of Camay. For a second soap stings and the cloying smell hits my senses and it's not too bad. Then the salty foam makes me retch and spit and reach for the water glass. I drink and spit out three full glasses of water, then clean my teeth with peppermint toothpaste to get rid of the taste. It seems to have worked. My mouth does feel fresher. I'll not fucking swear again. That's a joke.

Tonight I'm baby-sitting. Fiona has asked me to do this and I leap at the chance to do something for her, for both of them. They're going to some dinner at the university. John Kebler is in the sitting room when I get there. He's wearing a dark suit and a bright tie. He has a yellow silk hankie in his pocket. He has left off his glasses and his thick eyelashes are much in evidence.

'Very flash,' I say, nodding to the yellow hankie.

He takes it out, looks at it, and then shoves it in his trouser pocket. 'Sometimes you really do make me feel old and naff, Paulie.'

'That's a start,' I say.

Fiona comes in and even my breath is taken. Duckling into swan. Frog into Princess. The fucking lot! (So much for good resolutions about language.) The tangled hair has had a good brush and is held back by jewelled combs, floating behind her ears, gleaming and lovely. Her dress is a bias cut black sheath held up by shoestring straps and in place of chunky, grubby trainers she wears black stilettos with stacked soles. Around her neck is a simple necklace of small pearls.

'You look something else, Fiona,' I say. 'Great.'

'Kind of you to say, Paulie.' She blushes. Blushes! Just too fucking nice. And me I am lost to myself. Floating in a dead universe.

'Keeva's going off to sleep,' she says. 'There's a number by the phone. But you won't need it.'

She pulls on a big o camel coat of some age and grabs a brightly beaded bag. 'Thanks Paulie,' she says, smiling.

'A pleasure,' I say.

The door clicks behind them and I throw myself onto the sofa. 'A fucking pleasure, all right.' I start to think again about that girl who topped herself inside. Then I go to the kitchen to get some coffee to zap me out of those thoughts. Fiona has left a tray. Grapes. Stout ham sandwiches. A bottle of sparkling water. I make myself some coffee, then walk around the kitchen, poking into cupboards and under surfaces. I read postcards that have been sent to them from all over England. All over Europe. All over the world.

In one corner there's a stack of household bills, some paid, some unpaid. There are letters from Fiona's sister who lives in Paris, and from two ex-students of John Kebler's who are now doing research, respectively, in Oxford and Frankfurt. There are fragments torn out from newspapers that mention John Kebler and his great work. There are photographs of them both, alone and together. There is one with Keeva, one with an older tanned looking girl, the daughter whose room I now occupy.

I place these things out on the big kitchen table, spreading them out in a pattern that reaches the very edges. This is John Kebler and his Fiona. This is their web. It holds them in some kind of fragile tension with the outside world. It lets them know who they are, where they are and what really matters.

If I were to make a similar web for myself there would be newspaper articles about me then, when it happened, and now: other people inventing me for their own pleasure and fascination. There would be my slim volumes. Well - one slim volume. I could break open the volume, separate the pages and scatter them right across the table. Then would put Queenie and the others into my web. I don't have photos of my father and Jonno: the police took them away or they went missing somehow. Perhaps they burned in the conflagration. Perhaps I should reclaim that property. I suppose when I appeared to have murdered them both it would be improper for me to have their photos. Until I retrieve them I'd have to make do with the grainy images from the newspaper where they both look more like murderers than murderees.

John and Fiona's web is powerful - multi stranded, dense with mutuality. A web that can easily support the two of them, little Keeva and the stepdaughter in America. Just now, it even supports me. On the other hand my web could never compare with their web as it lies here on this table. My web is still fragile, insubstantial, and insufficient perhaps to support even this one whole human being.

A whimpering cry trickles down from upstairs. Very carefully I return the Kebler web to its notice board, to its heaps and to its piles. I return my own imaginary web to the fragile compartments in my head and belt upstairs.

The baby Keeva is whimpering, reaching out for the mobile that is rustling just above her head. I crank it and set it away and it creates its own hypnotic dance of dolphins and fishes, round and round. She chuckles and both hands come up, trying to reach them. Her fat hand catches mine and I hold onto it. 'Shsh,' I say. Shsh.' she knows it's me standing there. She knows I'm not Fiona. But she's OK. I would like a picture of Keeva on my web. She trusts me. Her eyes droop and her head turns to one side. I ease my hand out of hers and creep away.

Their bedroom is next to Keeva's. The door is half open so I creep in there, too. A ruched silk lamp casts a faintly pink light on the high chest that does service as a dressing table. The bed is roughly made. The room reflects the faintly organised chaos of the rest of the house- part of its style. You can tell his side of the bed from hers. His side table is neater: three books (including my slim volume), a spectacle case and a box of tissues sit alongside his mobile phone. I climb onto the bed and I lie where he must lie. Then I close my eyes and try to find some resolution to the ache I carry inside.

34 ENDING THE BEGINNING

The next day John Kebler catches me at the door as I set
out to buy some milk. 'There was a call from Maritza,
Paulie. She told me to tell you to get the Chronicle and
then ring back. I got the paper. Come in here.' To my
surprise he takes me into his pristine consulting room,
guides me to sit in one of the deep chairs by the window.
Then he hands me the newspaper, and goes to the window
and stands with his back to me.

He has marked a half page article entitled Knife
Attack on Welder, illustrated by a photo of a handsome man
in his mid-thirties. Beside it is a fuzzy photo of a face, large
boned and big nosed, of Christine Cazelet. The copy below
tells of a woman stalking the man, Seamus Rogers, for
several weeks, then breaking into his house and lying in
wait for him, before killing him with one of his own
kitchen knives. After that it seems that the woman called
Christine Cazelet had jumped into Mr. Rogers's own car
and driven it along the coast road and driven it right over
the cliff. A spokesman for the wife of the victim, Mrs.
Rogers, who was under sedation in a very shocked
condition, said that this was an unprovoked attack. She
said that although the family knew Miss Cazelet vaguely,
there was no reason for such an attack. A spokesman said
Miss Cazelet had been having treatment for stress and had
a history of mental disorder.

John Kebler comes and sits in the chair opposite. But he does not touch me. 'So what do you want to do, Paulie?'

I stare at him.

'Do you want to telephone Maritza? You could use this phone.' He pulls the telephone trolley into arm's reach. 'Shall I dial the number, Paulie?' He dials it and I can hear Maritza's voice at the other end of the phone. 'Paulie? Paulie?'

'Yes. Maritza. It's me.'

'Did you read the piece in the paper? Isn't it awful? Poor Christine. He was the one.' Maritza is breaking down in tears at the other end of the line. 'He was the one, you know, the one at the heart of all her trouble. Did things when she was little. Set it all away with her. He was the one.'

'Bastard,' I say. 'Fucking, fucking bastard.'

'But Paulie, he's dead, that man ...'

'At least she had her day.' What a cliché! Stewart Pardoe would have killed me for that. At least she had her day. But then he's dead too, isn't he?

'And now she's dead, Paulie. She drove off the cliff!' Maritza is snuffling and puffing on the other end of the phone. I remember how close she and Christine were in Brontë House. I can hear another voice in the background: 'Mam! Mam!'

'Is Sam with you?' I say. 'Get him to make you tea or something. I'll come round now to see you.'

'No. No, Paulie! Wait. I'm all right. Sam's here. I'll ring the police and ask about the funeral. Shall I? And let you know?' I hear her blow her nose. 'I'm all right, Paulie. I have Sam here. How about you? How are you? Are you alone?'

She has Sam. She has Amy. I look at the figure before the window, standing again with his back to me. 'There's someone here.'

She waits, but I don't tell her who the *someone* is. 'Look. Ring me tomorrow will you? I'll come and talk.' I click the phone back in the cradle. 'It's my fault,' I say.

There is a metal vice around my chest and my breath starts coming in short gasps. John Kebler keeps his back to me. I start to hit the arms of the chair. 'What's the fucking use? What is the fucking use? What is the fucking use in anything? Do you know in these last days I've been thinking of this girl who topped herself inside? How clean that was? What a solution? Now here's Christine. She had the right idea.'

He turns. 'No, Paulie. It was a solution for her, for the other girl too. It's not a solution for anyone else. Not for you.'

'Did you know? That this bloke, this Seamus, messed about with her when she was a kid? Messed her head as well, so she starts to run and cut herself.' I'm rocking backwards and forwards in the big chair. 'Compared with that, I suffered nothing. I only killed my mother when I was born, I only saw my father burned to extinction, watched my boyfriend destroy him. I've spent six years in an eight by ten cell. Even so I don't hate myself so much that I'd drive a car into the sea. Me, I don't even have that much courage.'

Now he's right at my side. 'Don't be ridiculous,' he says. 'These events have nothing to do with you.'

'If I'd gone to her straight away when I got out... We would have talked... She wouldn't have ...'

'Paulie, you couldn't find her. You can't live in might-have-been worlds. It could just be amazing that she has survived that long, given the pathology.'

'Fuck pathology!' I'm angry now. 'Don't you see?' I hiss. 'She was alone. I'm alone. I am entirely, entirely alone. I could have helped her. I am alone.'

'Nonsense. I am here. I'm here for you.'

'Oh no you're not! You're here for professional reasons. You're fucking guilty because six years ago you people didn't do your job right. If you had I wouldn't have been convicted. You're watching your back. I am just some case to you.'

His face is a mask. He looks older than his years. 'That is not true, Paulie,' he says grimly. 'This is personal and you know it.'

I know that with a certain look, a movement of my arms, I can bring him on his knees beside me. He will take me in his arms and tell me…

Why am I being tested like this? This is not fair. I put my hands on the arms of my chair and pull myself upright. 'I have to go,' I say. 'I promised to see Queenie today.'

'I'll run you.'

'No,' I say. 'I'll make my own way. I mean it!' Stiff legged, and with what dignity I can muster, I walk past him, through the door and down the stairs to my room. Down there I scrabble in my rucksack for a brown envelope that I was given at the prison gate. There's information in there about some resettlement agency. Maybe I'm not going to drive myself over a cliff. I don't have the courage for that. But at the very least I need to get myself out from under John Kebler's roof. Away from his gaze and the reach of his arms.

I take Queenie with me on the bus, back into town. On the way I try to tell her about Christine. She reacts quite strongly at first and then, losing interest, comments on the trees that brush the upstairs windows of the bus and the speed of the cars as they whizzed along the dual carriageway.

At one point on the cliff a section of the wall is marked with red and white tape and there is a police car on guard in the rain. A ripple of comment and a stretching of necks dart through in the bus like a shut-in bird.

'Is that where she did it?' says Queenie, suddenly. 'Is that where that child did it?'

Heads turn towards us.

'Yes, that's where the poor child did it,' I say.

At the resettlement place they are quite helpful. There might just be a one-person flat available, especially given my unfortunate situation. The officer had read all the details in the papers. 'Great shame, that. Good that they put it right.'

'My auntie here,' I nod at Queenie, 'I'd like her to be with me. Would that be possible?' Well, two bedroom flats are harder to sort, but the woman will see what they can do. And there is a possibility of work. One or two placements are possible, especially considering the nature of my case. 'Such a tragedy for you Miss Smith!' In the meantime she would help me with my social security forms… I have to grit my teeth to tolerate what is, after all, a kindly act. But here I am, parcelled and processed and being put through a system. I feel as though I'm back inside: an object of other people's action. Still, the woman smiles. 'We'll be in touch, Miss Smith.'

Then Queenie and I escape into the town like truants. We have tea in Fenwicks. We go to the furniture floor and sit on beds and chairs to try them out. We go to the hat department to try on a hat, and buy her one in navy, one in red. We choose those oversize cloches which are very much in this year, if you look at the magazines. Young faces stripped of expression model them with style. Queenie looks like an ancient child in her mother's hat.

Then Queenie gets tired again and we have another cup of tea.

'Would you like it,' I say to her, 'Would you like you and me to have a little flat? For us to live together?'

She is sitting perched forward on her chair in that little bird poses of hers. 'Together, dear? You mean I'll have the top bunk? Or do I still have to have the bottom bunk?'

My heart sinks just a little. 'But first we'll have to go to the funeral.'

'Whose funeral, dear?'

'Christine. You know. Christine's. She drove her car over the cliff. We saw the red and white tape, didn't we? I told you. Christine died.'

35 A VERY GOOD FUNERAL

Paulie: Five days later Queenie and I meet up with Maritza and attend Christine's funeral together. There's some comfort in the fact that I'm not here on my own.

The coffin is white, only barely polished wood. There is a modest service in the church and a bland address by a very young vicar, about young sacrifice and life well lived. His thin-toned self-conscious false-friendly chat rings hollowly in the church which is empty except for two women at the front and the three of us where we sit in the back row.

'Christine would have laughed,' whispers Maritza in my ear. 'The way that lad's going on. And this church! What a dreary place.'

The vicar loses his place and - horrors - Queenie stands up beside me and her reedy voice - projecting like an old style teacher's - pierces the air. 'She was a very kind girl, was young Christine. Always cheerful. She told us how to conduct ourselves in the prison. She knew the ropes. *You must not tell what you're in for.* That was important. That was a rule. She told us that in the van. And she told Paulie where to push the button when I wet myself. But to no avail. Using the button that is. They're better at my place now. But I still wet myself,' she said sadly.

A click of disgust pings out from the front row. One of the women, wearing a smart black hat, turns round; her heavily made up face is twisted in fury. This makes me get to my feet to say my piece. 'Christine had been in and out if prisons since she was a child. She knew prisons and other institutions inside out, so she could help all of us. She really helped us. She was a very brave girl and defended us. Christine was in prison through no fault of her own. It was not her fault that she was there. She was betrayed by others. But she had Great Spirit. Her laughter rang down the corridors. Her laughter was rebellion.'

There is a rustle behind us. Fucking hell. It's Lilah standing at the back in a swagger coat, an Asda carrier bag drooping from her arm. 'She was very kind. She plaited my hair in a hundred locks. And she fought for me when I was tormented. And she knew what it was like, to be under the blanket.'

Even quiet, demure Maritza is on her feet. 'She was brave and young and enduring. Sharing a cell with her helped me learn who I am. She protected the ones she loved, even up to death.'

Now Queenie is on her feet again. '*Suffer little children to come unto me.* That's what it says in the Bible. It also says, *Blessed are those who hunger and thirst after righteousness, for they will know the Kingdom of God.* "That was our young friend Christine, hungering and thirsting after righteousness. She will know God. Mark my words.'

A small figure suddenly emerged from behind Lilah, almost too small for an adult. 'My name is Tigger,' she piped up. 'Christine was my true friend. We had a laugh. We climbed trees together. She liked to be called by her proper name. Christine. Her name was Christine.'

And now we all clap and shout, like we used to sometimes inside, for the sheer joy of being alive. Extraordinarily, the vicar joins in. The younger woman of the two in the front is clapping too. Beside her, the older woman is staring at us with wide, hostile eyes.

At last the undertaker's men in not-quite-black suits pick up the coffin with their gloved hands and flip it up to their shoulders, a bit like coal miners flipping a bag of coal onto their backs. And the last of Christine Cazelet passes us down the aisle.

Outside the church we catch up with Lilah and the girl called Tigger and we all hug, hold each other as we never would have inside.

I say, 'She'd have like it that you came, Lilah.'

Lilah sighs. 'I saw it in the paper and I wanted to come. I told them at home I was at the shop. Extra shift.'

The younger woman from the front of the church comes and takes my hand, then Maritza's, then Queenie's, then Christine's, then Lilah's, then Tigger's. 'Thanks for coming,' she says. 'All of you. She'd have loved that shouting, laughed like a drain.'

'You're Sallyanne,' says Maritza. 'She told me about you.'

Sallyanne looks at us, one to the other. 'You know about this, don't you?'

Maritza nods. 'She told me you knew…'

'Yes. I'd have gone forward with her to tell the police about him. But my mother,' she glances at the other woman who is by the big black car, 'My mother went crazy. Said we were mad, vindictive. And our Christine wouldn't go forward without our mother agreeing because she said they'd have rubbished me like they rubbished her.'

230

'Did Christine live with you?'

Sallyanne sighs. 'She lived with me now and then. Sometimes in a squat. Sometimes back in prison. Sometimes in hospital. She still hurt herself. She loved my little girls. One of them's named after her, our Chrissie. She adored our Chrissie. Then a fortnight ago our Seamus picked up Chrissie from school and delivered her to my house. He was all smarmy smiles.' She shudders. 'Our Christine must have flipped about that.' She rubs her wet face with her scarf.

'Sallyanne!' The woman's voice cuts sharp as a knife through the air. 'Come on!' We see her well-cased bottom vanishing into the back of the limousine. Sallyanne raises her eyebrows, shrugs and smiles slightly and follows her.

The coffin has been loaded up onto the hearse and the vicar is talking to the undertaker. He comes across, rubbing his hands in the cold air. 'Well now,' he says. 'That was remarkable. A great tribute!' He shakes us each by the hand. 'Christine was unlucky in so many things but she was blessed in her friends.'

He bustles off, his gown ballooning in the air behind him. 'What a sad sight it is,' says Queenie thoughtfully. 'A man in a dress!' Then we all explode into laughter, holding each other up, shouting into the chilly air and the people on the pavement opposite look hard at us and clearly think we're raving mad.

We find a pub which doesn't look too full and sit round a table drinking and talking. Lilah has a full beef burger and chips and the rest of us steal her chips and talk about Christine, about ourselves. Tigger tells us about her and Christine in the residential school, and about what Christine said about being put into care by her mother. She

231

tells us about her own close shaves with the law. Then we get back to Christine again and it's as though she's here alive amongst us. In the end there is nothing more to say. We drift into silence, exhausted with grief and regret tinged with curious kind of satisfaction.

'Guess what! I'm going to live with Paulie,' Queenie suddenly says, cracking the silence. 'I'm going to have the bottom bunk. I said I didn't mind.'

Now here is my web: four women sitting clustered round a table clutching at the memory of a fifth woman. Stretching behind us are those taut parallels, our individual lives: tense fragile constructions stretched through dark spaces which have led with ineffable elegance to this round table on this wet afternoon. We are five women, counting Christine, webbed together now with shared experience, mutual respect and well won affection.

Outside in the rain a police car makes its urgent way, blue light flashing.

Ends

Also by Wendy Robertson-

Cruelty Games (1996)
Self-Made Woman (1999)
Where Hope Lives (2001)
My Dark Eyed Girl (2001)
The Long Journey Home (2002)
A Woman Scorned (2004)
No Rest for the Wicked (2005)
Family Ties (2006)
The Lavender House (2007)
Sandie Shaw and The Millionth Marvell Cooker (2008)
The Woman Who Drew Buildings (2009)
An Englishwoman in France (2011)
Knives Short Stories (2007)
Knives Short Stories 2:(2012)
Forms of Flight Short Stories 2013

WENDY ROBERTSON

Made in the USA
Charleston, SC
19 September 2013